Moonlight Mile

MARGUERITE HENRY'S

Ponies *of* Chincoteague

◆ Moonlight Mile ◆

CATHERINE HAPKA

Aladdin

New York   London   Toronto   Sydney   New Delhi

ALADDIN

An imprint of Simon & Schuster Children's Publishing Division

1230 Avenue of the Americas, New York, New York 10020

This Aladdin paperback edition April 2015

Text copyright © 2015 by The Estate of Marguerite Henry

Cover illustration copyright © 2015 by Robert Papp

All rights reserved, including the right of reproduction in whole or in part in any form.

Also available in an Aladdin hardcover edition.

ALADDIN is a trademark of Simon & Schuster, Inc., and related logo is a registered trademark of Simon & Schuster, Inc.

For information about special discounts for bulk purchases, please contact Simon & Schuster Special Sales at 1-866-506-1949 or business@simonandschuster.com.

The Simon & Schuster Speakers Bureau can bring authors to your live event. For more information or to book an event contact the Simon & Schuster Speakers Bureau at 1-866-248-3049 or visit our website at www.simonspeakers.com.

Book design by Karina Granda

The text of this book was set in Adobe Caslon Pro.

Manufactured in the United States of America 0315 OFF

2 4 6 8 10 9 7 5 3 1

Library of Congress Control Number 2014959031

ISBN 978-1-4814-0346-7 (hc)

ISBN 978-1-4814-0345-0 (pbk)

ISBN 978-1-4814-0347-4 (eBook)

◆ CHAPTER ◆

1

"BRR. IT'S COLD TODAY!"

Nina Peralt laughed and glanced at her friend Jordan, who was hand-grazing her horse a short distance from Nina and her pony. "Are you kidding?" Nina said, pushing a stray strand of curly black hair off her sweaty forehead. "It's got to be almost eighty degrees out here."

She scanned the broad, grassy expanse of the levee at the edge of Audubon Park. It was crowded with people as usual, while a few yards away, the lazy waters of the Mississippi sparkled in the late-afternoon sunshine.

"Actually, my friend Haley would say it never gets cold here in New Orleans," Nina added. "She lives in

Wisconsin, where it's positively frigid for, like, half the year."

"Haley? Oh, is that one of your *imaginary* friends?" Jordan giggled and gave a tug on the lead rope as her horse took a step forward to sniff at a patch of weeds.

Nina just laughed again. She was used to being teased about her far-flung online friends. A little over a year and a half earlier, Nina's parents had surprised her with a very special birthday gift: her pony, a stout bay pinto named Bay Breeze. Nina had already known Breezy, since he'd belonged to a family friend, and had even ridden him a few times. But it was only after he became hers that she started researching his special heritage as a Chincoteague pony.

That was when she came across three other girls her age in a horse-related chat room, all of them just as crazy about the rare pony breed as she was. Brooke Rhodes lived in Maryland, only a few miles north of Chincoteague, Virginia, and the neighboring island of Assateague, where Chincoteague ponies roamed wild and where all four girls' ponies had started their lives. Brooke had bought her pony, Foxy, at the yearly pony auction in Chincoteague, which Nina happened to think was the coolest thing ever.

Then there was Haley Duncan. She lived on a farm in Wisconsin and leased her pony, Wings, from a neighbor. Haley and Wings trained and competed in the challenging sport of eventing, and Haley's stories had inspired Nina to get more serious about her own riding. Even though she wasn't particularly competitive and didn't care much about winning prizes, Nina liked to challenge herself—and her pony—to be the best they could be.

Maddie Martinez lived in northern California and rode a pony named Cloudy at her local lesson stable. The pretty palomino pinto mare didn't technically belong to her, but that didn't make Maddie love Cloudy any less. In fact, it had been mostly Maddie's idea to start a private website to make it easier for the four Chincoteague-loving girls to chat and exchange photos. Nina had known immediately that it was a perfect plan. With the help of her mother, a professional artist, Nina had designed the site's layout and logo, while the other members had contributed computer expertise, written the text, and helped get the whole thing up and running.

The four girls had never met in person. But countless online discussions and occasional phone calls had made them the best of friends, and Nina couldn't imagine life without them—even if her local friends pretended not to believe they actually existed!

"Don't be a hater, girl," she told Jordan lightly, waving a hand to shoo away a passing buck moth. "I know you wish Freckles was a Chincoteague pony so you could join the Pony Post too."

Jordan glanced at her horse. Well, he wasn't technically *her* horse, though Nina thought of him that way. Freckles was a stout little Appaloosa gelding who belonged to Cypress Trail Stables, where both girls rode. Jordan had been leasing him for about six months, which meant she got to ride him as often as she liked.

"Whatever," Jordan said, giving Freckles a pat. "So are you and Breezy ready for the show? I'm not sure I am, you know? I think Miss Adaline wants me and Freckles to do a jumping class, and I just don't think we're ready for that. I mean, this will be our first real show!"

She sounded nervous. Jordan could be like that—she

often switched from happy and carefree to anxious or panicky or worried in the blink of an eye. But Nina didn't mind. Jordan's unpredictable changes of mood made her interesting, and Nina appreciated interesting people. Besides, she was good at jollying Jordan through her fears most of the time.

"I know. My first horse show too. But forget that for a sec," she told Jordan. "More importantly, what are you and Freckles going to wear for the costume class?"

Jordan's pale hazel eyes brightened. "I don't know yet. I mean, it was such a surprise I haven't even had a chance to think about it yet, you know?"

"Yeah, I hear you." But despite her words of agreement, Nina's mind was already filled with ideas for the costume class, which their riding instructor had announced after their lesson that day. The girls had already known about the horse show, of course—it had been on the Cypress Trail Stables schedule for ages. And their riding instructor, Miss Adaline, had mentioned that there might be a costume class when she'd first told them about the show over the summer. Somehow, though, in the flurry of going back to school and everything else, the girls had forgotten all about that part. So the official announcement of the special class had been a surprise.

"She said our ponies should be part of the costume," Jordan said. "That makes it trickier to think of ideas."

"But more fun, too," Nina added with a smile.

"Yeah, I guess." Jordan looked thoughtful. "You'll help me come up with something good, right? And then help with the actual costume, too?"

"Absolutely." Nina ducked to retrieve a stray bottle cap from the grass in front of Breezy's nose. He probably wouldn't eat something like that, but better safe than sorry. Nina's friends at the stable liked to joke that Breezy would try to eat anything that wasn't nailed down.

"Good. Because you know I'm not as artsy as you are." Jordan giggled. "I mean, if it was up to me, I'd probably end up cutting two holes in a sheet and going as a ghost rider or something lame like that."

A shout rang out from nearby, and Nina glanced over to watch as a group of college-age kids started chasing one of their friends, a skinny guy who was grinning and holding a bag of cookies up over his head. Both ponies ignored the ruckus—while a lot of horses might have spooked at the sudden commotion, it was nothing Breezy and Freckles hadn't seen and heard before. They were city ponies, stabled in busy Audubon Park, and accustomed to all sorts of things most equines never encountered. That meant passing the strange sounds and smells of the zoo, sharing the trails with pedestrians, dogs, bicycles, golf carts, and various other vehicles, and grazing on the levee, where they could encounter anything from a noisy pack of picnickers to a gaggle of cyclists to a huge barge passing by on the river, spitting out clouds of black smoke.

Nina's gaze returned to her pony, who was still nibbling steadily at the grass. Sometimes she wondered what Breezy would think if he were suddenly transported to Haley's rural family farm, where he could have a whole huge, quiet pasture to graze in all day long instead of a few bites of grass here and there and hay in his stall or a tiny dirt paddock the rest of the time. Even Brooke's smaller backyard field would probably seem like paradise!

Then again, Breezy would probably eat so much grass he'd

explode by the end of day one, Nina thought with a smile. *Besides, he loves this city as much as I do—he'd miss the action for sure!*

"Well?" Jordan's voice, slightly impatient, broke into her thoughts. "Any ideas? The show's a week from tomorrow, you know."

"I know. And don't worry—I work well under pressure."

"What were the costume categories again?" Jordan said. "I know Miss Adaline said there'd be prizes in a bunch of different ones, like prettiest costume and most creative, right? I think she said something about best local-inspired costume too."

"And scariest," Nina put in. "Can't forget that one, especially this close to Halloween."

Jordan shrugged. "Not that it's *that* close—I mean, Halloween is weeks away."

"Yeah." Nina grinned. "But that's okay. People here in New Orleans don't need Halloween or any other excuse to dress up and have fun, right?"

Jordan grinned back and lifted her hand for a high five. "For sure."

As the girls smacked hands, a jogger approached with a dog trotting beside him on a leash. The dog spotted the horses and started barking wildly at them. Freckles lifted his head to stare at the dog, but Breezy barely twitched an ear in its direction.

Jordan tugged on the lead to move her horse away a few steps, though Freckles had already lost interest and lowered his head to the grass again. "Maybe I could dress Freckles up as a dog," she said uncertainly, raising her voice over the barking. "And I could be, um . . . the person walking the dog?"

"Or the monkey riding the dog? Or the cat riding the dog?" Nina suggested with a laugh, watching as the dog's owner broke into a faster run, leading the barking beast away. "Could be cute. We'll put it on the list." She turned to stare at Jordan and her mount, sizing up the possibilities. "It would be fun to take advantage of Freckie's spots somehow."

"So the dog would be a dalmatian?" Jordan sighed and shook her head. "Actually, maybe I don't like the dog idea after all. I'd rather dress up as something pretty. Maybe a princess?"

"Okay. That's definitely an option—princesses and horses go together like red beans and rice." Nina rested an arm on Breezy's broad back, idly watching a skateboarder doing tricks on the path nearby. "But I bet a bunch of the girls will do the princess thing. Maybe we can come up with something a little more creative. A mermaid?"

Jordan looked interested. "How would that work?"

"Well, Freckles could be a fish. We could make him fins out of poster board or papier-mâché or something, and maybe paint his spots to look like scales. And you'd wear a mermaid tail and ride sidesaddle . . ." Nina let her voice trail off at Jordan's look of alarm.

"Sidesaddle?" she exclaimed. "I'm going to have trouble getting in enough jumping practice not to totally embarrass myself in the regular show classes! I'm not sure I can figure out *sidesaddle* at the same time!"

Nina laughed. "Okay, okay, don't panic," she said, tugging on Breezy's lead to keep him from wandering onto the footpath. "No mermaids. What about if you and Freckie both dress up as clowns? I think Miss A said there's a 'funniest' category."

"Eh, I don't know." Jordan shrugged. "I'm kind of scared of clowns."

"Even better." Nina grinned. "You could win funniest *and* scariest!"

"Ha-ha." Jordan stuck out her tongue at Nina, then shuddered. "No clowns."

"Okay, no clowns." Nina was staring at Freckles again. "Maybe you could be a Native American girl. I mean, Appaloosas were originally Native American war horses or something, right? And you'd look great with braids and a cute buckskin dress."

Jordan looked interested. "That could work, I guess. We could paint, like, symbols on Freckles or whatever."

"Of course, Native Americans didn't have saddles," Nina said. "You'd have to ride bareback. But that's okay, right? Lots easier than sidesaddle."

"I don't know." Jordan suddenly looked anxious again. "I mean, I've ridden him bareback before. But at a show? What if I get nervous and slide right off?"

"Well, maybe you could put a blanket over your saddle so it doesn't show," Nina said.

But Jordan was already shaking her head. "Maybe we should think of a different costume," she said. "What about a Mardi Gras theme? That would work for the local category."

"I like it!" Nina's mind quickly shifted gears, filled with images from the huge yearly celebration that had helped make New Orleans famous throughout the world. "One of my aunts collects Mardi Gras masks—I'm sure she'd let you borrow one. We could drape beads around Freckie's neck, and paint him to match your outfit . . ."

"Love it!" Jordan clapped her hands and grinned. "And you're such an expert vintage shopper, I bet we could find the rest of the stuff we need. . . ."

With that, they were off and running. Fifteen minutes later, Jordan looked happy and excited about her costume plans. "This will totally work," she declared, rubbing Freckles on the withers. "Thanks, Nina. But wait, what about you? Want to brainstorm some ideas for your costume?"

"That's okay." Nina shot her a coy smile. "I think I already know what I want to do. Don't want to talk about it yet, though—I need to let the idea simmer."

Jordan smiled back. "I bet it's something fabulous and creative that will win *all* the prizes, right? Okay, I won't ask, even though I'm dying of curiosity. I'll just say that if you're thinking of doing something for the scary category, you could ask Brett for ideas. He loves horror movies—he's probably seen every one ever made."

Nina turned her face into the breeze that was blowing in off the river, not answering for a moment. Jordan's comment had made all thoughts of costumes fly out of her head. Until recently, Brett had just been Jordan's one-year-older, slightly annoying brother. Nina had known him forever—they'd all grown up in the same neighborhood—though she hadn't really spent much time with him, since she went to a small private school over near the French Quarter while Jordan and Brett attended the local public school.

Lately, though, a couple of Nina's older friends kept mentioning how cute Brett was getting. And the thing was, Nina couldn't totally disagree. He sort of looked like one of the members of that new boy band everyone was talking about, and once she'd noticed that, she couldn't *un*-notice it. Did that mean she was turning boy crazy, like everyone said her cousin Charlotte had been at her age? Nina wasn't sure, and the thought made her feel off balance in a way she couldn't quite figure out.

"What time is it?" Jordan asked, breaking into Nina's confused thoughts. "I need to get home soon and start my history paper if I don't want to flunk out of school."

"It's . . ." Nina glanced at her watch, a funky vintage one she'd picked up at her favorite Magazine Street thrift shop. When she saw the time, she gasped. "Oh, wow," she exclaimed. "I told my mom I'd be home twenty minutes ago! I'm supposed to be helping her pack up for her art show, and—oh, never mind, I'll tell you later." Clucking to a startled Breezy, she took off at a jog in the direction of the stables. "Anyway, I've got to go!"

CHAPTER

2

NINA DASHED DOWN THE SIDEWALK ALONG
Magazine Street, dodging hurrying shoppers and strolling tourists. A stout middle-aged woman looked up from sweeping the stoop in front of a flower shop.

"Nina! Where you at, darlin'?" the shopkeeper called. "Haven't stopped to see me in ages!"

"Soon, Miss Vera, promise!" Nina called back without slowing her pace.

An elderly man was sitting on the steps of the next shop reading a newspaper. He chuckled as Nina dashed by. "Running to meet your boyfriend, Miss Peralt?" he asked.

This time Nina slowed just long enough to blow him a kiss. "You know you're the only man for me, Mr. Otis," she said as she took off again, the old man's chuckles fading behind her.

Finally she reached her street, barely slowing her pace for the sharp turn off Magazine and thus nearly running into a young mother pushing a baby stroller. Nina dodged just in time.

"Sorry, ma'am!" she called as she passed.

"No worries, Nina," the woman, a neighbor from the other end of the block, called back. "Your mama was looking for you just now."

"I know, I'm late—thanks!" Nina tossed over her shoulder.

A few steps later and she was home. The charming century-old cottage was the only place Nina had ever lived. Her parents had bought it for a song the year her father graduated from law school, mostly because it had a courtyard in the rear where her mother could work on her sculpture in the fresh air. The rest of the place had been a mess, at least according to the stories Nina's aunts, uncles, older cousins, and grandparents delighted in retelling every chance they got. Falling-down walls, leaky pipes, cockroaches the size of a Chincoteague pony—the tales got taller every time, but that was how it went with her father's side of the family. In any case, in the years since, Nina's parents had transformed the interior into a bright, modern, art-filled space, though the outside retained every bit of its vintage appeal, the only real changes being a fresh coat of paint and an energy-efficient bulb in the antique porch light.

As Nina was about to push open the metal gate and climb the steps onto the small front porch, she spotted a familiar figure hurrying toward her from the other end of the block. It was her father, his long limbs flapping and his briefcase slapping against his side.

"You're late!" Nina called with a grin.

"I know, I know." He was out of breath as he reached her and leaned in for a quick peck on the forehead. "Hey, Boo. Your mother's going to kill both of us, eh?"

"Probably. We promised to be home like half an hour ago." Nina sneaked a look at her watch as her father pushed open the sky-blue door, leading the way inside.

When Nina followed, the first thing she heard was loud meowing as the family's two Siamese cats, Bastet and Teniers, appeared as if out of thin air to wind around her legs and demand attention. The second thing she heard was even louder cursing coming from the back of the house.

"Uh-oh." Her father dropped his briefcase on the rosewood console table beside the front door. "Sounds like she started without us."

"Yeah." Nina scooped up Teniers and hugged him despite his yowl of protest. "Sorry, kitty babies. Your dinner will have to wait." She dropped the cat beside Bastet and hurried through the kitchen and down the narrow back hallway after her father.

Her mother's studio was a converted bedroom at the very back of the house, where the sun came in through two large windows and a row of French doors leading into the courtyard. The room had built-in shelves along one wall, while the rest was mostly open and dotted with bits and pieces of work and rolling bins of equipment.

Sheets of oilcloth covered the wooden floorboards beneath half-finished clay sculptures. A few finished pieces were sitting on a long, well-worn table with a chipped marble top that stood near the French doors, awaiting transport to the local foundry, where they would be cast in bronze or other materials.

Nina's mother was at the table now, along with the family's longtime maid, Delphine, a petite and energetic woman who proudly traced her ancestors back to one of the French *casquette* girls who had arrived in New Orleans in the 1700s. The two of them were bent over a piece on the table. It was a medium-size sculpture that Nina's mother had been rushing to finish the past few weeks, a modernist portrayal of several women laughing and cooking together. The shapes and details were fluid and rather abstract, like most of Nina's mother's work, but Nina could tell that the women in the piece had been inspired by her aunts and cousins.

At the moment, Nina's mother and Delphine were grasping the base of the clay sculpture, clearly planning to hoist it off the table and into the large wooden crate sitting on the floor near the door. From past experience in helping her parents move similar pieces, Nina guessed that the thing had to weigh at least fifty or sixty pounds.

"Hang on!" Nina's father exclaimed, striding forward. "Let me help."

"Yeah," Nina said at the same time.

She didn't notice that the cats had followed her to the studio. As she stepped forward, the toe of her paddock boot landed squarely on Teniers's tail. The cat squawked loudly and shot forward—just as Nina's mother took a step, staggering slightly under the sculpture's weight.

"*Non, non!*" Delphine said. "I need to—"

She never finished the comment. Teniers crashed into Nina's mother's legs, tripping her just as she took another unsteady half step.

"Ack!" she exclaimed as the sculpture jerked out of her grasp. Delphine tried to hang on to her half, but it was no use.

"Careful!" Nina's father yelped.

CRASH!

The sculpture landed upside down, squashing the soft

clay of the top half of the piece. The intricate figures were reduced to mostly shapeless blobs.

"Oh! Oh!" the maid cried, her hands flying to her face. "The ladies—they are ruined!"

Tears sprang to Nina's eyes. All that work!

"Oh, Mom," she exclaimed. "I'm so sorry! This is all my fault—if I hadn't been late—"

"Me too," her father added, stepping forward to encircle his wife in his long arms. "I'm sorry, love."

"No, it's all right." Nina's mother sighed, then smiled slightly, leaning against her husband for a moment before pushing him away and stepping over to examine the fallen sculpture. "I mean, it's not *all right*," she amended, poking a chunk of clay with a bare toe. "It's pretty much trashed. I should have guessed something like this would happen. Things have been going a little too well lately, what with landing this big solo show and all. . . ."

Nina's father chuckled. "Uh-oh," he said. "Don't tell me my family is finally rubbing off on you, Eva? I thought your Yankee sensibility would never succumb to Big Easy superstition."

Despite what had just happened, Nina couldn't help smiling at that. Her father's family had lived in New Orleans pretty much forever—or at least since the time of the Louisiana Purchase. While his family and Delphine's both considered themselves Creoles, most of Nina's father's ancestors had come from Africa or the West Indies rather than France or Spain, and they'd brought their own beliefs and ideas with them. For generations, the family had steeped in the great melting pot of New Orleans culture, with its mishmash of traditions, including plenty of superstition and voodoo. By now, of course, most of the family treated such things as nothing more than local color—fun to talk about at parties, but nothing to take too seriously. Nina and her father certainly fell into that category. But a few family members still believed, at least a little, including Gramma Rose and Uncle Oscar.

Nina's mother, on the other hand, had grown up in a voodoo-free subdivision in suburban New Jersey. She'd come to New Orleans on vacation soon after graduating from art school, met Nina's father in a jazz club, and never left. Even though she'd been there for more than fifteen years now, her in-laws still loved to tease her about her sensible Yankee ways.

"Maybe so," Nina's mother said with a small smile. "I just know I've had this feeling that something bad might be coming."

"Don't say that, *madame*!" Delphine crossed herself.

Nina's father laughed again. "Better watch out, Delphine," he joked. "Sounds like Great-Aunt Serena might be hanging around these parts."

Nina's eyes widened. *Weird,* she thought. *I can't remember the last time Dad mentioned Great-Aunt Serena . . .*

"Stop, Gabe." Nina's mother tried to look stern, though there was a twinkle in her blue eyes. "I'm just saying, maybe this was meant to be. In any case, you all don't need to look so upset—it's not a big deal."

"How can you say that?" Nina squatted beside the sculpture, poking gingerly at what remained of one of the figures. Teniers wandered over and rubbed against her knee, purring loudly, and she tapped him on the head. "Naughty Teniers!"

"No, seriously," her mother said. "Teniers probably did me a favor. I was feeling pretty ambivalent about that piece anyway."

Nina looked up at her. "What do you mean?"

Her mother shrugged. "I mostly rushed it out for the show. I didn't really even stop to think about whether it was working. And in the end, well, I'm not sure it was. It's really pretty similar to some of my past work." She smiled ruefully. "I'd hate to have the critics accuse me of being derivative of myself."

"But I thought you needed that piece to fill the show," Nina's father said.

"True. But maybe I can use something else," Nina's mother replied. "I've got plenty of older pieces that haven't been out in public yet." She winked. "Could be fun to figure out which one fits."

Her husband looked thoughtful. "What about that piece on the breakfront? I've always liked that one. . . ."

Bastet had wandered into the room by then too. She head-butted Nina, letting loose with a piercing Siamese yowl. Leaving her parents discussing their sculpture options and Delphine bustling around putting away the wooden crate, Nina headed back toward the front of the house to feed the cats. Once that was done, she went to her room to change out of her riding clothes.

Nina's room lay between the kitchen and the studio. It was the smallest bedroom in the house, but she didn't mind. Her parents had let her decorate it however she liked, and she'd treated it as her own personal art project, adding and subtracting things over the years. The walls were each painted a different color and the door was covered in a collage of photos and sketches of family, friends, and beautiful spots throughout the city. Instead of ordinary curtains, Nina had draped the two narrow windows with Mardi Gras beads. The rug beside the bed had been a gift from her cousin DeeDee after a trip to Morocco. Her bedspread had been handmade by her great-aunt Shirley.

Nina knew her room looked different from those of most of her friends, but she'd never understood the appeal of going to the mall and buying shiny new things with no history at all. What was the point of having stuff without a story?

There were horsey touches too, of course—Nina had been fascinated by horses for as long as she could remember, though she'd only been riding for a few years. She'd created a handmade frame out of driftwood, stones, and bottle caps for her favorite photo of Breezy. Above her bed hung a slightly faded Victorian print of a pair of Arabian horses running wildly through the night. It was spooky and a little weird, and Nina had loved it from the moment she'd spotted it in the back corner of a local junk shop, though it had taken her a couple of months to save up her allowance to buy it. One of her mother's sculptures, a horse rolling luxuriously in the dirt, stood atop the whitewashed bookshelf. Beside it, in a place of honor, was Nina's copy of *Misty of Chincoteague*.

Nina patted the book's well-worn cover as she hurried past on her way to the overstuffed wooden wardrobe where she kept most of her clothes. She dug out a pair of leggings and a funky beaded tunic she'd found at a flea market. Once she was dressed, she flopped onto her bed and grabbed her laptop off the bedside table. It was Friday, which meant dinner with the relatives. Nina guessed they'd be leaving as soon as her parents cleaned up the mess in the studio. But first, she wanted to make some notes on her costume idea while it was fresh in her mind.

She forgot about that when she logged on and saw an alert message flashing on her desktop. Oops! She'd totally forgotten that she'd arranged to "meet" the other Pony Posters for a chat that day.

Normally the members just left messages for one another whenever they could. With the four of them living in three different time zones, it was rare for more than one or two to be on the site at once. But every so often they liked to get together in real time, all four of them. Today was supposed to be one of those times.

"Sorry, guys," she murmured under her breath as she quickly brought up the site.

As expected, the other three were already there. Nina scanned the messages. There were already several new ones. It wasn't long before Nina spotted her name.

> [MADDIE] OK, so are we taking bets on how long it'll take Nina to remember to show up? Lol!

> [BROOKE] Give her a few more minutes. Maybe she was late coming home from the barn.

> [HALEY] Ya, pretty sure she had a lesson today.

> [MADDIE] I know, I'm just teasing. But she'd better show up soon!

"I'm here, I'm here," Nina said aloud. She quickly opened a text box and started typing. A moment later she hit enter and her message appeared below the others.

> [NINA] Sorry I'm late! Lost track of time, etc., boring blah blah.

[HALEY] It's OK—ur here now!

[NINA] Thx! Anyway, I have news: found out something fun at the barn today. There will be a costume class at my horse show next Sat!!!

[MADDIE] Cool!

[BROOKE] Yah. U said something about that a while ago, right?

Nina should have known that Brooke would remember, if anyone did. She was probably the quietest of the bunch, and at first that had made Nina feel as if she didn't know her quite as well as the others. But after a while, she'd realized that Brooke's mind was always working double-time even if her mouth—and typing fingers—could be a little slow. "Still waters run deep," Gramma Rose always said. It had taken Nina a while to figure out what that saying meant, but now she thought of Brooke whenever she heard it.

[NINA] Miss A said something about the costume class a while ago, but then we all forgot. So it was like a whole new surprise, lol!

[HALEY] So u and Breezy both dress up for the class?

[NINA] Right. And I already know exactly what our costume will be, and I'm super excited about it!!!

[BROOKE] Don't keep us in suspense!

[HALEY] Ya—spill!

[NINA] Give me a chance to type it out, lol!

[MADDIE] OK, but hurry! Dying to know more!

Nina nodded and typed as fast as she could, her slim fingers flying over the keys. Finally she hit enter and sat back to watch her message appear.

[NINA] I'm going to dress as an ancestor of mine. Her name was Serena, and she lived around the time of the Civil War. She had a totally tragic life. Her fiancé joined the Buffalo Soldiers and ended up dying of cholera. According to old family stories, Serena never got over it. They say her unhappy, restless spirit haunts her descendants to this day—when everything is going perfectly right, she steps in to make it go horribly wrong.

As she scanned what she'd written, Nina's mind drifted to her mother's sculpture. But she shook off the thought. Serena was a fun family legend, nothing more. Ghosts weren't real.

[HALEY] Whoa! Cool story!

[MADDIE] And cool costume idea! Esp. so close to Halloween.

[BROOKE] Totally. So what's Breezy's role?

• 31 •

[NINA] He's going to be Serena's

ghost horse, of course!

[MADDIE] Duh, B. What, did u think Breezy was

going to dress up as Serena's dead boyfriend, lol?

[BROOKE] ha ha, OK, fine. So did the

real Serena have a special horse?

[NINA] No clue. But everyone rode back

in those days, right? It'll be fine. I already

have some cool ideas about how to

make Breezy look super spooky—like

braiding some gray and silver ribbon into

his mane and tail, and turning his coat

gray and ghostly with something. Talcum

powder? Hmm, will have to experiment.

[HALEY] I'm sure u will come up w/something!

U are the most creative person I know.

Before Nina could respond, she heard her father calling her name. "Oops," she said, glancing at the vintage cat clock on her wall. Its hands were stopped at two thirty, since Nina was always forgetting to wind it. But she didn't need a clock to know it was time to head out to meet her relatives.

[NINA] Sorry guys, I have 2 go. Family dinner.

[BROOKE] O right, it's Friday.

[MADDIE] Talk to u soon. Let us know how the costume is going!

[HALEY] And take lots of pics!

[NINA] U know it. Later guys!

◆ CHAPTER ◆

3

"KEEP HIM MOVING, JORDAN! DON'T LET him be lazy!" Miss Adaline called.

Nina held her breath, watching as Jordan gave Freckles another kick. The pair was heading toward a small cross-rail in the middle of the ring. Nina's riding class was more than halfway through their Saturday morning lesson, and they'd just spent several minutes jumping the obstacle from a trot and a canter. Now, after all five riders had jumped it a couple of times, Miss Adaline had decorated the standards with fake autumn leaves and added a row of small pumpkins underneath the rails.

"All the jumps at the show will be decorated," the

instructor had explained. "We don't want your horses to be surprised by seeing something different. Successful showing is all about preparation." Miss Adaline was a cheerful woman in her late twenties who liked to tint her chin-length dreadlocks different colors—this month an autumnal orange. She was also one of the best riders Nina had ever seen, competing not only in the hunter/jumper style she taught the students at Cypress Trail Stables, but also in saddleseat riding.

Jordan was the first rider to try the newly decorated obstacle. Normally Freckles was a steady, reliable jumper. But when he neared the jump, his ears pricked forward at the pumpkins.

"Push! Keep his attention!" Miss Adaline hollered.

"Go!" Jordan blurted out, giving her mount one more kick a couple of strides out.

The Appaloosa spurted forward, and Nina thought he was going to put in an extra-big jump. Instead he darted left at the last moment, ducking out and around the fence! Jordan wobbled and lost her stirrups, but managed to stay in the saddle.

"Sorry!" she cried, her face flaming as she fished for her flopping stirrups.

"Don't apologize," Miss Adaline said briskly. "Just circle back and give it another try. This time, keep your left leg and left rein on him so he doesn't think he can do the same thing again."

Jordan nodded, shortening her reins and taking a deep breath. Nina shot her an encouraging smile and a thumbs-up as Freckles passed at a rapid trot.

"Go, Freckie," whispered the rider beside Nina, a slightly older girl named Marie. She was astride her own pretty gray mare, but Nina knew she'd leased Freckles before Jordan.

Freckles slowed down again on the approach to the fence. But this time Jordan kicked him more determinedly. The horse hesitated slightly, then hurled himself over the fence and cantered away smoothly.

"Way to go, girl!" Nina cheered.

Miss Adaline smiled. "Yes, much better," she said. "Nina? You're up next."

Nina nodded and gathered up her reins. "Wake up,

Breezy," she said, squeezing with both calves. "Our turn."

She sent the pony into a trot. He felt sluggish at first—Breezy liked to take any opportunity he got for a quick nap. But Nina had plenty of energy to spare, and she urged him forward with her legs, seat, and voice. By the time the pony circled toward the fence, he was moving along nicely.

Like Freckles, Breezy pricked his ears at the pumpkins. But all Nina had to do was squeeze and cluck, and one ear swiveled back toward her. His trot never faltered. A moment later he was cantering away after a smooth jump.

"Nice!" one of the other girls in the class called out.

"Yes, lovely," Miss Adaline agreed. "Marie? Give it a go."

Nina gave Breezy a pat as she rode to the end of the line. Jordan twisted in her saddle and smiled.

"Way to go!" she whispered. "Those crazy decorations didn't scare Breezy at all, huh?"

"Nope," Nina whispered back. "I guess once a pony swims the Assateague Channel, it takes a lot to scare him!"

Jordan giggled, and Nina gave Breezy another pat. She

was proud of her pony. With the show only a week away, the riders were all a little nervous—and their horses had obviously picked up on that. Marie's mare had overjumped the crossrail even before the decorations went up, while one of the other horses had refused to canter the first three times his rider tried.

But Breezy had been his usual calm, consistent self. *I'm a lucky girl,* Nina thought as she watched Marie's mare veer back and forth several times before finally launching herself over the jump with about two feet to spare. *My Breezy Boy is practically perfect!*

The rest of the lesson went just as well for the pair. By the time Miss Adaline called for the girls to dismount, Nina was smiling from ear to ear.

"You were awesome, Breeze-man!" she murmured into his ear as she ran up her stirrups. "That show next week is going to be a blast!"

She shivered as she thought about it, though she wasn't really nervous. Nina didn't usually get stage fright, since she'd been performing in dance recitals almost from the time she learned to walk. Performing in a horse show couldn't be that different, right? If anything it would be easier, since she'd have such an amazing partner doing most of the work.

Besides, she didn't really care whether they won any ribbons at the show. That wasn't what it was about for her. All she cared about was letting everyone see what a spectacular pony she had!

Normally, English was one of Nina's favorite classes of the day. For one thing, the teacher liked to do lots of dramatic class readings of the books they were studying, and Nina loved acting out different roles and pretending to be all kinds of other people. Besides that, the class took place in the dormer room of the old Greek Revival mansion that had been transformed into Nina's small private school. It was fun to sit there and imagine all the interesting sights that had passed in front of these windows over the many years since the house was built.

On this particular Tuesday afternoon, though, she wasn't thinking about any of that. As the teacher gave the homework assignment, Nina sneaked a peek at her watch, wondering if the school day would ever end.

Finally the final bell rang. Nina leaped to her feet, shoving her books into her battered canvas tote as she hurried toward the door. She headed straight for her locker, where she found her friend Trinity waiting for her.

"Ready to shop?" Trinity asked eagerly. She was a tall, lanky girl with auburn hair and freckles that dotted her face and body as thickly as stars in the Milky Way. Trinity hated those freckles and was always plotting ways to rid herself of them, but Nina thought they made her friend beautiful and unique.

"I'm ready," Nina said. "Jordan's meeting us at the corner of Magazine and Harmony."

The two girls joined the stream of students pouring toward the exit. Soon they emerged into the sticky afternoon sunshine.

"Streetcar or cab?" Trinity asked.

Nina consulted the clock on the bank across the street. "Streetcar," she said. "We have time. And I want to save my money for costume stuff."

"And coffee, right?" Trinity said. "I'm not trekking all

the way over to your part of town without hitting Jojo's."

Nina laughed as she headed for the streetcar stop. "For sure."

As soon as the two girls settled onto the streetcar's wooden bench seat, Trinity turned to face Nina. "So are you ever going to tell me what your costume is?" she asked, raising her voice above the clunk and clatter as the streetcar rattled down the tracks. "Otherwise even a super-talented shopper like me is going to have trouble helping."

"Soon," Nina promised. "Jordan's been waiting since Friday to hear; she'll never forgive me if I tell you first!"

Trinity didn't stop trying all through the slow ride along St. Charles Avenue, just as Nina had expected. That was exactly why she hadn't told her about this shopping expedition until that day at lunch—Trinity was probably the least patient person Nina knew, and an expert wheedler and whiner. But she was also an expert shopper, and Nina knew she'd help her and Jordan find exactly what they needed for their costumes.

They got off the streetcar at Eighth Street and hurried down toward Magazine, cutting across to Harmony halfway there. Nina moved fast, partly because Jordan was always early and partly so Trinity would be too busy trying to keep up to bug her about the costume. When she emerged onto Magazine, Nina spotted Jordan right away. She was leaning against a brick wall watching a couple of kids argue over some candy.

Jordan spotted Nina, too. "You finally made it!" she exclaimed, hurrying toward them.

"Chill, we're early." Trinity collapsed against the wall, digging into her bag for her lip gloss. "Anyway, just so you know, Nina told me all about her fabulous costume idea on the way here."

"Stop, I did not!" Nina gave Trinity a playful punch on the arm. "You know I wouldn't do that to you, J."

"At this point, I don't even care," Jordan said. "Just tell me already!"

"Yeah, spill, Peralt," Trinity added.

Nina grinned. "Okay. So you know my family's lived in New Orleans forever, right? Well, way back in the Civil War days, we had this ancestor . . ."

She went on from there, telling the two girls about

Serena. As she talked, Jordan's eyes went wide.

"Oh my gosh," she said when Nina finished. "I'm so not sure this is a good idea."

"What are you talking about? It's genius!" Trinity grinned. "So we're basically looking for, like, some ghostly Civil War–type rags or something, right?"

"Pretty much." Nina glanced at the vintage shop across the way, the reason for their meeting spot. "Although I can do the rag part myself—if we can find something that can pass for the right era, I'll make sure it looks ghostly and tattered, as if the wearer has been wandering the wild wasteland between the worlds for years and years." She wiggled her fingers spookily at her friends.

Jordan shuddered. "Stop!" she said. "Are you sure you want to do this? You just said Serena likes to punish people in your family when they get too happy. Don't you think she'd also punish someone who uses her life story to try to win a costume class?"

Nina laughed. "You sound like my grandma," she said. "Come on, let's shop. This place might have some stuff for your costume too."

Jordan still looked uneasy. But she followed Nina and Trinity across the street and into the shop.

"Nina!" The shop owner looked up from folding a stack of antique handkerchiefs. She was a small woman in her fifties with close-cropped graying hair and cat's-eye glasses hanging on a chain around her neck. Nina had known her all her life, since she'd been friends with Nina's mother even longer than that.

"Hey, Miss Marie," Nina greeted her. "Happy Tuesday."

"Same to you, darling." Marie's round face and enormous smile made her look like the Cheshire cat. "Remind me, Nina, when's Eva's show again? I want to make sure I'm there to cheer her on."

"Starts weekend after next," Nina said. "I know she'll be happy to see you there."

Marie jotted a note on the calendar beside the old-fashioned cash register, then perched her glasses on her nose and peered at all three girls. "Looking for something special today, ladies?" she asked.

"Just browsing," Jordan said.

Nina nodded. "We're looking for costumes, but we're

of the family had scattered across the city and surrounding areas.

The weekly family dinners were always fun, no matter where they took place. But that night Nina was a little distracted. She'd been working hard on her costume all week. In her riding lesson that afternoon, Miss Adaline had kept things simple and easy, telling the students she didn't want to wear out the horses before the big day. Afterward, Nina and Jordan had taken their mounts for a quick graze on the levee, though they'd left earlier than usual to put the finishing touches on their costumes.

All I still have to do tonight is finish dyeing my gloves, she thought. *Then I should get to the barn early to set up the stuff I'll need to turn Breezy all ghostly. . . .*

"So Nina," Kim said, breaking into her thoughts. "Your horse show is tomorrow, right?"

Nina nodded and took a sip of water. "It starts at ten," she said. "I can't wait."

"We can't wait to come and cheer you on," Tommy's wife, Brandy, told her. "The kids are really looking forward to it."

not quite sure what we're looking for," she explained.

The shop owner pursed her lips. "I understand. Half the fun is in the search, hmm? Just let me know if I can help."

She went back to her work as Nina and her friends headed deeper into the shop. "Okay, let's spread out," Trinity said briskly. "We have a lot of stores to cover today."

Marie's shop was crammed with treasures. It was tempting to stop and examine everything that looked interesting, but Nina tried to stay focused. There wasn't much time to pull two costumes together, and she wanted them to be perfect. So she barely paused over a gorgeous tie-dyed tank top, and only held up a cool old sundress in front of her instead of trying it on.

Still, she didn't find anything that seemed right for her Serena outfit, or for Jordan's Mardi Gras costume either. Finally she pushed past a rack of plus-size dresses to get to the back corner of the store. That was where Marie usually kept what she called "oddities"—pieces that didn't really fit anywhere else. Nina wasn't sure what she might find there that would work for either her costume or Jordan's, but she could never resist taking a peek at that rack. It was where some of her favorite finds had come from, including her fringed poncho and a cool embroidered vintage apron she'd turned into a lampshade.

This time there wasn't much on the oddities rack—just a couple of bathrobes, a fake fur coat, and a few other things. Nina was about to turn away when she noticed beige fabric peeking out from behind the fur.

"Wait, what's this?" she murmured under her breath, pushing aside the coat.

She gasped when she saw what was there: a pair of old riding breeches. Trinity heard her and peered over a rack of shirts.

"What'd you find?" she asked. "Something good?"

"Something spectacular." Nina pushed her way out into the main part of the store, clutching the hanger. "Check it out!"

She held up the breeches. Trinity grabbed them for a closer look. "Wow, these look pretty old."

By then Jordan had heard them and wandered over. "Are those riding pants?" She wrinkled her nose. "They smell kind of musty."

"I can take care of that." Nina grabbed the breeches back from Trinity. "I'm going to try them on."

"You mean for your costume? Would Serena have worn that?" Jordan trailed after her toward the tiny dressing room in the opposite corner of the store.

"Not for the costume." Nina pushed aside the paisley curtain and stepped into the dressing room. A precarious stack of shoe boxes stood in one corner, making it even smaller than usual. "For the regular part of the show," she called out through the curtain as she peeled off her pants.

"You're going to wear those in the *show*?" Jordan sounded faintly horrified. "But—"

"Perfect!" Nina sang out as she pulled on the breeches. "Well, close enough to perfect, anyway."

She stepped out to show her friends. Trinity glanced up from digging through a pile of jeans and nodded. "Very cool," she declared. "Very retro. I like."

Jordan looked less convinced. "Are you sure you want to wear those in the show?" she said. "It'll make you look, you know, different."

"Exactly." Nina smiled at her friend, knowing that

Jordan always struggled to understand Nina's love of being different, unique, interesting. "I was thinking my show outfit seemed kind of boring. I mean, navy jacket, white shirt, black boots—where's the fun, right? These will give it the perfect touch!"

"If you say so." Jordan still looked dubious. But she didn't say anything else, probably because she'd known Nina long enough to know it was pointless to argue about stuff like that.

Meanwhile, Trinity was already turning away. "Change back, Neens, and let's move on," she tossed over her shoulder. "I fully approve of impulse buys, but we can't get too distracted. And I don't see anything that'll work for either of your costumes in here."

Trinity kept them moving nonstop for the next hour plus, hitting every suitable shop within a ten-block radius. They found harlequin-print pants and a purple blazer for Jordan's costume, and a floaty gray tunic top for Nina's. Finally, as they left yet another resale shop with bags in hand, Jordan gestured to the coffee shop across the street.

"I'm dying of thirst," she said. "Let's take a break."

"Exactly what I was about to say," Trinity agreed, leading the way.

Nina wasn't going to argue. Jojo's Brew was one of her favorite hangouts. She and Jordan had spent countless hours there doing homework, gobbling down delicious, freshly made beignets, or just gossiping over steaming cups of coffee or frosty iced tea.

When they walked in, the place was packed and echoing with talk, laughter, and clinking spoons. Even in the crowd, Nina spotted Brett immediately. He was perched on a stool at the narrow counter by the front window, flanked by several friends Nina vaguely recognized from the neighborhood.

"Oh, good," Jordan said as she spotted her brother. "He owes me money—now I won't have to borrow from you guys to pay for my drink. Hey, Brett!"

Brett glanced over his shoulder. When he saw them, he leaped up and hurried over, leaving his friends behind.

"Hey," he said, shoving both hands in his jeans pockets. "What's up?"

Nina returned his smile, feeling self-conscious. "Hey," she said. "You know Trin, right?"

"What's up?" Brett glanced at Trinity and nodded. "So you guys had a caffeine craving too, huh?"

"You owe me five bucks." Jordan held out her hand. "Pay up, okay?"

Brett dug some crumpled bills out of his back pocket. "Whatever, here," he said, glancing at the bags the three girls were holding. "Let me guess, you spent the rest of your money on shoes and hair ribbons and stuff." He grinned, obviously finding his own joke hilarious, though Jordan just rolled her eyes.

"Don't you ever listen when I talk?" she complained. "I spent like half of breakfast telling Mom how we were shopping for costume stuff today."

"Oh, right, the horse thing." Brett shrugged and laughed. "I keep waiting for you to give up on that and take up a real sport."

Jordan frowned at her brother. "Riding is a real sport," she retorted. "You'd know that if you had the guts to try it."

"Nah, I'm not a fan of prancing around in tight pants and playing with ponies." Brett grinned at Nina. "Speaking of ponies, I hear you and your runty little spotted thing are doing this show too, huh? Hope he can see over the top of the jumps!"

Nina wasn't easily annoyed. Not usually, anyway. For some reason, though, Brett's words made her feel defensive of Breezy. Typical boy—Brett obviously thought that her pony's modest height had something to do with his abilities.

"We're doing it, all right," she snapped, ignoring her friends' surprised looks. "And we're going to win every class we enter, too!"

• CHAPTER •

"PASS ME SOME MORE OF THAT SHRIMP, would you, Nina?" Uncle Oscar patted his belly. "Still got a little room left in here, I think."

"If not, he'll make room!" Nina's cousin DeeDee barked out a laugh and elbowed her longtime boyfriend, Tim, who was sitting beside her, shoveling down his second helping of Gramma Rose's potato salad.

Nina grinned and grabbed the dish between her and her grandmother, passing it across the table to her uncle. It was Friday night, and this week the family dinner was at Aunt Toni and Uncle Elijah's place, a comfortable but rather small shotgun house in Bayou St. John. It was a full house that week, which meant about twenty members of Nina's father's family were crowded around two tables in the front room, including Nina's four aunts and uncles, all six of her first cousins, and various spouses and significant others. Most of the little kids—Nina's young second cousins, who numbered nine so far, with one more on the way soon from Cousin Jeremy and his wife—were eating in front of the TV in the bedroom, though baby Ella was on Grandpa Jack's lap while her mother, Nina's cousin Charlotte, took a break from feeding her.

Nina was the only person in the house between the ages of seven and almost-thirty, but she was used to that. Her father was the youngest—by almost fifteen years—of Grandpa Jack and Gramma Rose's five children. At forty-one he was the same age as his oldest niece, Nina's cousin Kim. Nina's dad had grown up with Kim and Kim's brother, John, and Nina's cousin Tommy, who were all within a few years of the same age. From all accounts, they'd spent their childhood running wild throughout the Seventh Ward, where Gramma Rose and Aunt Vi still lived, though the rest

Tommy chuckled. "I'm still not sure it's a good idea to let them that close to the ponies. I hear riding lessons are expensive."

"You're telling me," Nina's father said. Everyone laughed at that.

Nina's mother helped herself to more salad. "Did we tell you all that Nina and Breezy are entering a costume class at the show?" she said. "Nina's been working on her costume all week."

"That's right." Nina's father smiled. "And I think some of you already know who she's dressing up as."

Cousin Kim nodded. "Nina told me all about it at dance class on Wednesday," she said. Kim was a dance instructor at a local studio and the main reason Nina had been dancing for most of her life. Before taking up riding, Nina had spent several afternoons a week and at least one weekend morning at the studio. These days, between Breezy, school, and other activities, she was down to once a week, but she still loved it. She'd taken classes in just about every style Kim offered, and was currently taking a contemporary class.

Grandpa Jack looked up from tickling the baby. "Don't keep us in suspense," he said in his raspy voice. "What's the costume, Nina?"

Nina glanced around the table. Aside from her parents and Kim, the only ones she'd told about her idea were DeeDee and Tim, since they'd stopped by the day before while she was working on the costume in the front room.

"I'm dressing up as Great-Aunt Serena," she announced.

"Serena?" Aunt Iris exclaimed. "What a terrific idea!"

Most of the others nodded, but Gramma Rose raised an eyebrow and Uncle Oscar frowned. "Are you sure you want to do that, Nina?" he said. "You know what family legend says about Serena—she can be vengeful."

Nina's cousin Jeremy laughed. "Here we go," she said. "Okay, Gramma. Your turn—tell us how it's unwise to mess with the spirit world."

Gramma Rose pursed her lips. "It's true," she told Jeremy, sweeping her gaze around to include everyone. "I know most of you don't believe it—"

"That's because most of us have joined the twenty-first century," DeeDee put in with a smirk.

"Or at least the twentieth!" Aunt Vi added.

"It'll be okay, Gramma," Nina said. "I'm being respectful. I just think it's cool that we have such a colorful ancestor. It's like a tribute, you know?"

"That's right," Kim said. "I think it's cool too."

Meanwhile Charlotte's husband, Paul, looked confused. "Hang on," he said. "Who's Great-Aunt Serena? Is she the distant cousin who lives in Biloxi?"

"No!" Aunt Toni laughed. "And don't let Cousin Tilly hear you think she's that old!"

"Serena was actually our great-great-great-aunt, I think." Aunt Toni glanced at Gramma Rose. "Is that right, Ma?"

Gramma Rose nodded. "That's right."

"She lived around the time of the Civil War," Charlotte told her husband. "I'm sure we've mentioned her before. . . ." With help from the rest of the family, she filled him in on Serena's life story.

As they finished, Uncle Oscar was shaking his head, making his jowls shake. He glanced at the window, where bright moonlight was filtering in through the sheer curtains.

"It's a full moon tonight, you know," he said in a somber voice. "Some believe that's a time of great supernatural power, especially for black magic and voodoo."

"Oh, come on now, Pop!" DeeDee rolled her eyes. "Serena was just a poor sad woman who lost the love of her life. That doesn't make her a voodoo queen or something— no matter how many tall tales our family likes to tell!"

Uncle Oscar folded his arms over his chest. "Well then, how do you explain the weird things that have happened in this family over the years?" he challenged his daughter. "Like the disaster at Great-Uncle Lou's wedding—"

"Or the way John cracked his head open trying to keep up with the younger guys from the office on the basketball court that time, right?" Cousin Kim elbowed her brother. "Yeah, I'm so sure that was Serena and not Jumping Johnny's own pride at work!"

"John's concussion aside, there have been plenty of incidents that can't be explained," Gramma Rose said. "My mother told me her grandfather's brother was badly injured when his horse spooked at nothing on the way to a party being held in his honor—even though by all accounts he was an excellent rider who never fell off."

"So what are you saying?" DeeDee shook her head. "Good old Serena figured a party was too much fun and decided to punish him? Yeah, right . . ."

Nina listened, nibbling on her potato salad, as the family discussed that incident and several more. She'd heard all the stories before and always enjoyed them.

"I've got a new one for you," she put in after Uncle Oscar finished recounting the legend of some long-dead relative's ruined business. "Serena's messing with Mom now!"

"Eva?" Gramma Rose glanced at her. "What happened, dear?"

Nina's mother looked up from her plate. "Nina's just joking around," she said. "I dropped a piece I was getting ready to enter in my show next weekend."

"And you said it was probably Serena's work," Nina reminded her with a grin. "She thought you were getting way too successful, so she broke your sculpture!"

"Hmm." Aunt Vi raised an eyebrow. "That's as may be. But speaking of your show, Eva, how are you coming along? It's only a week away now, yes?"

"Yes. I'm ready except that I still need to decide which piece to substitute for the broken one. And for some reason I'm feeling indecisive." Nina's mother shrugged. "I keep going over it, but I'm having trouble settling on which piece to use."

Aunt Iris looked up from her shrimp and rice. "I know which one I'd pick," she said. "You should use the one you did when Nina first got her pony. It's of the two of them riding in the moonlight. Remember?"

Nina tilted her head, trying to figure out which sculpture Aunt Iris meant. Her mother had sculpted her countless times, of course, and Breezy a few. But Nina didn't remember the one Iris had described.

"Which piece is that?" She glanced at her mother, who looked thoughtful and a little sheepish.

"I'm not even sure where that one is," she said. "Nina, I meant it as a surprise gift for you that Christmas, but I put it away and forgot about it. Remember, Gabe?"

"Not really," Nina's father admitted, spearing a bit of potato on his fork.

But Nina's mother was nodding slowly, gazing into

space without seeming to hear him. "But you're right, Iris, that one just might fit in the show. I should try to find it and see if it turned out as well as I remember."

"Good." Aunt Iris looked pleased. "Anyway, we're all looking forward to opening day next Saturday."

"Thanks." Nina's mother reached for the water pitcher. "But first we've got Nina's show to look forward to tomorrow. And don't forget, Gabe's band has a gig right down the street tomorrow night—hope you'll all be there, too."

"We wouldn't miss it," Charlotte said. "Got the babysitter all lined up."

Nina nodded. She'd almost forgotten about that gig. Her father was an attorney by profession, but he also played in a jazz band with some friends. They were all amateurs, but they were pretty good and often landed gigs at local spots. Nina made a mental note to invite Jordan and some of her other friends to come with her to hear his band play the next evening. It would be the perfect way to celebrate and blow off steam after the horse show!

◆ ◆ ◆

Nina was pulling on her nightgown when her cell phone buzzed. She picked it up and saw a text: a friend from school inviting her to see a late movie that night.

Sorry, Nina texted back quickly. *Going to bed soon—got to get up way too early tmw. Rain check?*

She sent the text and then turned off her phone. It was tempting to accept the movie invitation, but she'd already turned down several other activities that evening. She definitely wanted to be fresh for show day.

Especially since I told Brett we were going to win all the ribbons in sight, she thought ruefully. What had come over her that day at the coffee shop? She wasn't the type of person to get all worked up about stuff like competing and winning. She also wasn't the type to let other people's comments get under her skin—especially since she was pretty sure Brett had just been joking around.

But she shrugged and tried to forget about that. It was too late to worry about it now. Besides, Brett hardly ever came to Jordan's lessons. He probably wouldn't even show up tomorrow.

She stepped to the window and looked out. The full moon made everything outside look silvery and magical. For a moment Nina recalled her uncle's comments about Serena and shivered.

Hearing a rustle of movement from the doorway, she turned just in time to see Bastet wander in with Teniers right behind her. Both cats leaped gracefully onto Nina's bed, settling themselves in their accustomed spot at the foot. Nina smiled as they started to purr, then turned to check the duffel and garment bags sitting near the door. She'd packed everything she might need in there, including the costumes for herself and Breezy. The vintage breeches were sitting at the top of the unzipped duffel, and Nina stroked the rough beige fabric.

"I wonder who else might have worn you in a big show?" she murmured.

She gave the breeches one last pat, then grabbed her laptop and climbed into bed. Soon she was logging on to the Pony Post. Her friends there had been following her progress on the Serena costume all week, offering suggestions and encouragement. Nina had posted a photo of the breeches, too, promising to send them another picture of herself wearing them in the show ring, since her father was playing photographer tomorrow.

Now she found recent messages from all three of her friends:

[BROOKE] Good luck tomorrow Nina! Can't wait to hear all about it!!!

[HALEY] Me too! I know u and B will do great!

[MADDIE] Me three!!! Go get em, tiger! (That's what my dad says before my soccer games sometimes, lol!)

[MADDIE] O, and I know u say u never get nervous. But if u do, just picture all the other horses and riders in their underwear!

Nina laughed and opened a text box, typing fast.

[NINA] OK, now I'm totally picturing Breezy
dressed in boxer shorts and a tank top! Maybe
I should rethink our costume, lol . . . Anyway,
u guys are the best cheering section ever! I'll
let u know how it goes as soon as I can.

• CHAPTER •
5

THE SHRILL WAIL OF NINA'S ALARM YANKED her out of a restless sleep the next morning. She sat up and slapped it off, feeling tired and a bit fuzzy-headed. She'd noticed she often had especially vivid dreams during a full moon, and last night had been no exception. The difference was that this time, all the dreams had been about Serena—at least Nina thought they had been. The details were already fading, drifting just beyond reach of her memory, leaving her with only an unsettled feeling and the faint whiff of voodoo.

"Whatever," she said aloud, then yawned. She stretched her feet out beneath the covers—the cats had left, though not long ago since she could still feel the warm spot where they'd been.

Nina stood up, her nose twitching at the enticing scent of coffee drifting back from the kitchen. She glanced at the window, and for a second it was as if she could still see the full moon hanging heavy in the bright early-morning sky. But she shook that off, along with her lingering grogginess. The sun was up, and it was time to get this day started.

Cypress Trail Stables was always a pretty busy place, with an active lesson program and lots of boarders and leasers coming and going seven days a week. But Nina had never seen it as crowded and crazed as on this particular show morning. Miss Adaline and the other instructors were bustling around, helping students get ready. Horses stood in the wash racks or grooming ties, while riders raced back and forth to the tack room or their storage lockers.

Nina paused in the entryway for a moment, taking it all in. Jordan rushed past, holding a bucket, then stopped short when she saw her.

"Nina! You're finally here!" she said breathlessly. "Did you bring your costume?"

"Of course." Nina patted the duffel under her arm. "Got my show clothes to change into later too. That way they won't get dirty while I'm getting Breezy ready."

"Oh!" Jordan's eyes widened with alarm as she glanced down at her own pale gray breeches and white shirt. "Wish I'd thought of that. I'll probably be filthy by showtime."

Nina shrugged. "Don't worry. With my luck, Breezy will blow a big green pony sneeze all over me as soon as I change." She grinned. "Then again, maybe not. I'm feeling positive, since I've already got my lucky undies on."

Jordan laughed. "Seriously? You mean those ratty old pink things with the dancing teddy bears printed all over them?"

"Absolutely." Nina winked. "That's the best thing about those vintage breeches—the old-fashioned fabric is so thick there's no way anything will show through!"

Jordan just shook her head. "Honestly, sometimes I don't even know if you're joking or serious," she said. "But never mind—can you help me get the dirt off Freckie's fetlocks?"

"Sure. Just let me drop my stuff by Breezy's stall first."

For the next two hours, Nina barely stopped moving. She helped Jordan, then fetched Breezy out of his stall and gave him the grooming of his life. She wanted him to look perfect for his show debut.

"Twenty minutes to showtime, everyone!" one of the instructors hollered, charging down the barn aisle. "Make sure you're ready when your division starts!"

"Yikes." Nina glanced down at her shorts and T-shirt. "Better get changed, Breezy. I don't want to embarrass you by looking less fabulous than you do!"

She gave Breezy a brisk pat, which made him jerk his head up from his hay pile and let out a loud snort. He turned his head and eyed her rather suspiciously before stepping over to the stall door to look out.

Nina chuckled as she watched his ears prick this way and that. The hustle and bustle of show day had him—like all the horses and ponies in the barn—a little more jazzed than usual. After a moment, though, he returned to his hay pile, settling down to eat with one last sigh. Nina let herself out of the stall and headed for the changing room.

Less than ten minutes later, she was fully dressed in her show clothes, including the vintage breeches. A couple of people had already commented on the cool old pants, which made Nina smile.

She found Jordan by her horse's stall, looking pale and rather clammy. "Oh my gosh, I'm so nervous I could die!" she wailed. "My legs are shaking so bad, I don't think I'll be able to ride!"

"Chill. Breathe. Try not to hyperventilate." Nina rubbed her friend's arm, then grabbed Jordan's wrist to check her watch. "The littler kids still have one more division, then we're next. You'll probably relax once you start your warm-up."

Jordan raised an eyebrow. "Have you *met* me?" she exclaimed.

Her words came out sounding so wounded that Nina couldn't help giggling. For a second Jordan looked annoyed; then she blinked and started giggling too.

"Sorry," she said. "Am I spazzing out again?"

"Totally. But it's okay—it's one of my favorite things about you." Nina slung an arm around her friend's shoulder and gave her a hug. "Come on, I'll help you get Freckie's bridle on."

A few minutes later Jordan and Freckles were in the smaller riding ring, which was being used as a warm-up area. At least a dozen horses and ponies were in there, going every which way as their riders put them through their paces or jumped the small crossrails set up in the middle. Nina watched the action for a second, then realized she needed to start her own warm-up if she wanted to be ready. Breezy might be a little pepped up by the show atmosphere, but she wanted to have plenty of time to make sure he was moving off her leg and paying attention. Even a show probably wasn't enough to wake him up entirely!

Jordan glanced over, and Nina tossed her a thumbs-up. Then she turned and dashed for the barn.

As she raced in, she almost crashed into someone coming out. "Sorry!" she blurted out. "I was—oh! Uh, hi, Brett."

"Hey, Nina." Jordan's brother grinned at her. "I like the monkey suit."

Nina glanced down at her navy blue jacket and crisp white show shirt. "What, this old thing?" she said. "It's just what I wear around the house. You know."

Brett laughed loudly. "Good one!"

Nina smiled back weakly. The joke had been pretty lame, but she supposed boys were easily amused. "So you came to watch Jordan's show, huh?"

"I guess." Brett glanced around the barn. "The parentals insisted. I mean, it's not like I wanted to spend my Saturday smelling horse poo, you know?" He barked out another laugh at that. "So are you and the runt riding in the same, you know, competition thingy as Jordan?"

"Same classes, yeah." Nina smiled tightly, deciding to ignore the not-so-appreciated nickname for Breezy. "Speaking of which, I need to go get ready."

"Oh. Yeah. Good luck or whatever." Brett shoved his hands in the pockets of his faded jeans. "See you out there."

"Okay." Nina brushed past him and then stopped, not sure for a second where she was supposed to be going. Oh, right—Breezy. She turned and headed for her pony's stall, shaking her head at her own airheadedness. What had gotten into her lately? For some reason, being around Brett made her feel tongue-tied and strange.

But never mind—she didn't have time to worry about that right now. She reached Breezy's stall, unlatched the door, and swung it open.

"Ready to go, Breeze-man?" she sang out. "Let's go show 'em what we've got!"

Five minutes later, Nina was swinging into the saddle just outside the warm-up ring. Breezy normally stood stock-still for mounting—maybe almost a little *too* still, since Nina usually had to give him a couple of kicks to get him moving. Not that day, though. As soon as her left foot hit the stirrup, she felt the pony's weight shift. "Easy, boy," she said, quickly swinging her right leg up and over. As she did, Breezy hopped forward, and Nina collapsed heavily into the saddle to avoid overbalancing.

"You okay?" Miss Adaline asked, hurrying over from nearby, where she'd been helping another rider adjust his stirrups.

"Yeah," Nina replied breathlessly, shoving herself into position and tucking her right toe into the stirrup. "He just took me by surprise, that's all. He's not exactly his usual lazy self today." She gathered up her reins. Breezy had stopped, though he still felt a little tense.

Miss Adaline smiled. "The horses know it's a big day too. Don't overdo your aids—he'll be on his toes and probably won't need as much pressure as usual."

"Got it." Nina took a deep breath. "Here we go!"

Miss Adaline gave Breezy a pat on the neck, then stepped out of the way. Nina nudged the pony with both heels, expecting a sluggish step at most. Instead, Breezy practically leaped forward, and for a second Nina thought he might actually trot off instead of walk.

She laughed. "Okay, I get it, pony boy," she said. "Easy with the aids, like Miss A said, right?"

Breezy flicked one ear back at her, then turned it forward again as a tall black horse trotted past. As soon as Nina asked him to move off, Breezy swung into a ground-covering walk—the kind of nice, forward walk it usually took Nina about half a lesson to get out of him.

This is kind of nice, she thought as they rode through the gate and joined the flow of traffic in the ring. *If Breezy's actually going to volunteer some energy today, I might as well sit back, save my leg muscles, and enjoy it!*

She and Breezy were trotting a few minutes later when she heard someone calling her name. Glancing toward the rail, she saw Trinity standing there, waving.

Nina waved back, then rode over. "Hey, Trin, you made it!" she exclaimed. "Did anyone else come?"

"Yeah, the gang's all here." Trinity waved a vague hand in the direction of the bleachers and lawn chairs set up near the main ring. "Livi, Chelle, the whole bunch from school." She shaded her eyes and peered out at the crowd of horses and ponies in the warm-up ring. "Is that Jordan?"

Nina glanced over her shoulder. Freckles was near the middle of the ring, trotting a sloppy circle. "Yeah, she's a little nervous." Seeing Jordan made her think of Brett. Her gaze wandered over the crowd, wondering where he was.

She didn't see him, but she did spy a large crowd of familiar-looking people heading her way. She smiled and waved as her father, at the head of the group, spotted her and lifted his hand. Nina's mother was right behind him, along with Gramma Rose, Aunt Toni, Cousin DeeDee and Tim, Cousin Tommy and his three kids, and several others.

Soon the whole group was at the rail, greeting Nina and Breezy and saying hello to Trinity.

"This is so exciting!" Aunt Toni exclaimed, reaching out to give Breezy a pat on the nose. "Nina, it's like you're in the Olympics or something!"

"Maybe not *quite* like that." Nina laughed. "It's fun, though, right?"

Just then a horse cantered past right behind them, and Breezy jumped and turned halfway around. "Oh!" Gramma Rose cried. "Nina, are you all right?"

"I'm fine." Nina gave her pony a nudge to turn him back toward her family. "Breezy's just a little excited, that's all."

"Oh, dear." Her grandmother looked worried. "I hope you'll be safe out there, Nina."

"Don't worry about me." Nina smiled. "Breezy will take care of me."

"Yeah, relax, Gramma," DeeDee put in. "Nina's a pro at this riding stuff."

"Hmm." Gramma Rose looked unconvinced, though she reached up to give the pony a careful nose rub.

"Anyway, I should probably finish my warm-up now," Nina said. "And you guys should find seats. I think my first class starts soon."

"All right." Her father reached over the fence to pat Nina's leg. "We'll be cheering you on, Boo."

"Thanks." As her family hurried off, Nina gave Breezy a little kick to get him moving again. "Oops," she said as he sprang into motion, this time breaking into a brisk trot. Deciding to go with it, Nina closed her legs against his side, steering him into the flow of traffic as his stride lengthened.

After a moment she passed Jordan, which made her think about Brett again. She glanced out toward the seating area, wondering where he was and if he was watching her right now.

What? Why would he be watching me? she chided herself. *Stupid!*

Still, her eyes swept the crowd. Her family was easy to spot, moving as a large, boisterous group toward a free section of seats. She also spotted Trinity's red cloud of hair. But she didn't see Brett anywhere. . . .

"Whoops!" she blurted out as Breezy made a sudden turn to one side to avoid a horse that had stopped just ahead of them.

Both of Nina's feet slipped out of the stirrups at the unexpected move, and she clung on with her legs to keep her balance. Taking the squeeze as a request to go faster, Breezy broke into a canter.

"Whoa, baby," Nina said. Luckily she'd kept her grip on the reins, and she tightened them to slow her pony. "Trot—now walk."

Breezy obeyed, and Nina was able to get her stirrups back. She glanced around, hoping nobody had noticed her wobble. *Lemons into lemonade,* she told herself, smiling at the thought of her grandfather's favorite saying. *A little embarrassing, but a good reminder to pay attention.*

"Here we go," Nina whispered, feeling a flutter of excitement deep in her gut. She and Breezy had just stepped into the main ring for their first jumping class. The show was being run as a hunter competition. Each division consisted of four classes—three jumping rounds and a group flat class. This first round was meant to start things off easy. The jumps were lower than those Nina had been practicing in lessons lately, and the course was simple and inviting, with no sharp turns or tricky distances.

We've so got this, she thought as she nudged her pony into a canter. *Breezy could do a course like this in his sleep! In fact, half the time I think he does!*

She almost giggled at the image of Breezy snoozing as he cantered over a jump. But she swallowed her laughter and reminded herself to focus.

They completed their opening circle, then headed toward the first obstacle, a small vertical decorated with cypress branches. Breezy pricked his ears at it a few strides out, but his steady canter never faltered. He met the jump in stride, sailing over easily, and Nina grinned. This was fun!

The next two jumps went just as well. Breezy landed on the correct canter lead and loped around the turn, and Nina glanced over her shoulder toward the next line. As she did, something outside the ring caught the corner of her eye, just for a split second: a flash of movement, the flutter of something ghost-gray and wispy, like a tattered sleeve . . . For just that one moment, a flashback to her dream overwhelmed her, and she swore she smelled mothballs and wood smoke. . . .

What was that? she wondered, turning her head to look. *Probably just a horse's tail or something . . .*

As her eyes searched the crowd, she felt Breezy's stride wobble slightly. Quickly turning her attention back to what she was doing, Nina saw that the pony was veering to the left side of the jump. Was he thinking about running out, as Freckles had done in their lesson the other day?

They were only two strides out by now—not much time to correct their course. Nina kicked sharply with her left leg, tugging on the right rein at the same time. Breezy tossed his head and leaped to the right, his stride choppy. He was back in front of the jump now, but crooked and moving a little too fast.

"Go, Breezy!" Nina cried, kicking with both legs.

But it was too late. The pony tossed his head again and slammed on the brakes, almost sliding into the rails as he skidded to a stop.

Nina had already been leaning forward in anticipation of the coming jump; she was flung onto the front of the saddle and had to scramble to stop herself from sliding off over Breezy's shoulder. Somehow she shoved herself back into her seat, fishing for the stirrups she'd lost and grabbing for her reins as they slipped onto his neck. Her face flamed as she heard a sympathetic "Oooooh" go up from the watching crowd.

"It's okay, Nina!" Miss Adaline's voice floated out from the rail. "Circle and try again."

Nina nodded, already turning Breezy away from the jump. She kicked him back into a canter, looping back around to approach the jump again. This time she kept him firmly between her hands and legs, and Breezy cleared the jump nicely.

The crowd cheered as they cantered on to the next jump, but Nina's mouth was set in a grim line. *I can't believe I did that!* she thought. *Totally my fault. Breezy and I are supposed to be working as a team, and I just abandoned him right before the jump. So much for making my pony look good. . . .*

She shook her head to banish the thought, not wanting to get distracted again. Luckily, Breezy wasn't easily flustered, and he recovered quickly from the stop, completing the rest of the course with no trouble at all.

"Nina!" Jordan hurried over with Freckles trailing behind her at the end of his reins as Nina rode out of the ring. "Oh my gosh, what happened?"

"I spaced out," Nina said with a sigh, giving Breezy a pat. Then she forced a grin. "Actually, I should probably blame it on Great-Aunt Serena."

"What?" Jordan's eyes widened. "What do you mean?"

"Nothing." Nina smiled and shook her head as she slid down from the saddle and ran up her stirrups. "Something I saw outside the ring distracted me, that's all." Her gaze wandered toward the area where she'd seen the flutter of gray. What had it been? There were no horses over there, and nobody wearing gray, either.

Jordan followed her gaze, still looking alarmed. "Do you really think—"

"Absolutely not." Nina cut her off with a laugh, reminding herself that this was real life, not some moonlight-fueled dream. "Anyway, Serena might have gotten us this time, but Breezy and I will make up for it in our next round!"

• CHAPTER •

6

"READY TO GET BACK IN THERE, BREEZE-man?" Nina said as she checked her pony's girth.

She glanced toward the ring, where riders were already entering for the flat class. All the horses and the riders in their division would be asked to walk, trot, and canter for the judge, who would be watching the quality of the animals' gaits. Since this show was supposed to be a learning experience for the students, the judge would also add or deduct points for the riders' position and use of aids, even though the rider wasn't normally judged in a hunter class.

Nina had already all but forgotten that disastrous fence in her first jumping round. The other two courses had gone smoothly, and she thought she and Breezy might still have a shot at a ribbon if the flat class went well and the judge liked the pony's gaits.

"And of course she will, right?" she whispered into Breezy's ear as she adjusted his bridle. "Who could resist you?"

Breezy snorted, blowing out a splattering of yellow pony snot. Nina jumped back just in time to avoid it. She glanced down at her vintage breeches and laughed.

"You almost got me that time, Breezy," she said. "Now come on—let's get in there."

She led him to the mounting block and swung aboard. Miss Adaline was busy helping Jordan straighten her saddle pad, but Nina didn't really need any advice anyway. Walk, trot, canter—how hard could it be? They'd done mock flat classes in several of their lessons leading up to this show, so Nina knew what to expect.

Leaving her reins slack, she nudged Breezy into a walk, once again enjoying his extra energy. Steering with her legs, she aimed him toward the ring gate. Breezy snorted again and dodged half a step to one side as a cute little chestnut mare passed by in front of him. Nina laughed.

"Settle down, you nut," she said fondly. Leaning forward, she rubbed his neck, which was damp with sweat. "If I didn't know better, I'd swear you were some kind of fire-breathing—"

She didn't get to finish the comment. At that moment, something small and gray zipped past, inches from his front hooves. A split second later, a larger gray-and-white shape dashed after it in hot pursuit.

Cat, mouse. The words barely had time to cross Nina's mind when she realized Breezy was spooking violently sideways. She grabbed a chunk of mane with one hand, scrabbling for the reins with the other. But it was too late—Breezy was bolting forward, galloping toward the ring with his head in the air. Nina managed to hang on and stay in the saddle, but just barely.

"Look out!" someone yelled as Breezy careened into the ring, almost crashing into a stout draft cross standing just inside.

"Sorry!" Nina blurted out, still trying to reel in the reins. "Breezy, whoa! Stop!"

The pony didn't seem to hear her. A horse kicked out at him as he raced by, and Nina heard the rider cry out. All around the ring, people were stopping their mounts or spinning away to get out of their path.

Finally Nina managed to gain enough balance to haul back on the reins, bracing herself on the stirrups. That finally seemed to get Breezy's attention. He slowed, the wild gallop turning into a canter and then a choppy, high-kneed trot.

"Nina!" Miss Adaline had rushed into the ring. She jumped forward, catching hold of Breezy's reins.

At that, the pony finally stopped. His head drooped, and his sides heaved.

"Oh, wow," Nina said in a shaky voice. "Thanks."

She cast a quick look around at the mayhem she and Breezy had left in their wake. Several riders had dismounted, including Jordan, whose face was pale. One girl, a younger rider Nina didn't know, appeared to be crying as she clutched her pony's reins.

"Sorry about that, everyone!" Miss Adaline called out. "Everything's under control. We'll start the class in a moment." Then she glanced up at Nina. "You okay?"

"Fine." Nina forced a smile, though it felt as fake as Aunt Vi's fingernails.

"Okay, let's get him walking and make sure he's okay." Miss Adaline gave a tug on the reins to start Breezy moving. "I'll stay with you for a minute."

Nina was about to tell her she didn't have to do that; she could manage her own pony. But she bit her tongue and nodded instead. "Thanks," she said.

As they walked slowly around the ring, Nina told her instructor what had happened. "It's so not like him," she finished. "Since when does Breezy spook at something so silly?"

Miss Adaline shrugged. "Any horse can spook at anything at any time," she reminded Nina. "That's why we always have to be thinking riders."

"Yeah." Nina knew she was right. Still, it was strange. Once again, she felt a twinge of that dream sneaking into her mind.

But she did her best to shake it off as the announcer called for the class to start. True, it wasn't like Breezy to spook at a mouse. But it wasn't like Nina to think there was some spooky supernatural reason for it either.

No such thing as ghosts—duh! The thought made her smile, which made her feel better. Miss Adaline hurried out of the ring, and Nina sat up straighter in the saddle, keeping Breezy walking along the rail as she waited for the first command.

Jordan was waiting just outside when Nina rode out of the ring. The flat class had just ended. Nina and Breezy had done pretty well, though Nina had been extra cautious with her aids, and as a result Breezy had been a little slow to pick up the canter each time. She hoped the judge wouldn't count that against them too much.

"Hey," Jordan said. She'd already dismounted and run up her stirrups. "That was pretty wild what happened with Breezy. You okay?"

"Yeah, no worries." Nina filled her in on the cat-and-mouse story.

"Wow," Jordan said. "Breezy doesn't usually spook at stuff like that."

"No kidding." Nina didn't say anything else. She was still in the saddle, and over the heads of the people and ponies milling around, she'd just spotted Brett heading their way.

A moment later he was there. "Hey, Sis," he said, grinning at Jordan. "You managed not to panic and fall off. Congrats."

Jordan made a face. "Gee, thanks."

Brett had already turned away to peer up at Nina. "I liked your entrance," he said. "Very dramatic. Do you get extra points for that?"

"Yeah, I wanted to catch the judge's attention," Nina quipped ruefully, swinging her right leg over her pony's back to dismount.

RRRRRRRIP!

Nina tried to stop herself, to get her rear end back in the saddle, but it was too late. Momentum carried her over and down to the ground, where she staggered slightly on landing. Nearby, she heard Jordan gasp loudly.

"Nina!" Jordan stage-whispered. "Your pants just split!"

Duh, Nina wanted to say. But her entire body, including her mouth, seemed to be frozen. All except her eyes, which darted toward Brett's face. He was staring, his mouth agape and his eyes wide.

Then he gulped and spun away. "Uh, gotta go," he muttered, taking off into the crowd.

Finally Nina could move again. She dropped the reins, and both hands flew to her rear end. Just as she'd feared— just as she'd *known*—the entire back seam of her vintage breeches had split, leaving her lucky underwear on display for all to see.

"Go," Jordan hissed, grabbing Breezy's dangling reins. "I've got him."

Shooting her friend a silent look of thanks, Nina kept both hands where they were as she sprinted for the barn.

"Come on, dude." Trinity leaned against the wall of Breezy's stall, arms crossed over her chest. "You've got to do it. You worked so hard on your costume!"

"I can't go back out there." Nina didn't lift her gaze from Breezy's back, which she'd been brushing obsessively for the past five minutes. "I can't."

More than an hour had passed since her pants had split, and her lucky underwear was now safely ensconced in the black breeches she'd brought to wear with her Serena costume. But every time she thought about what had happened, Nina's face flamed as if it was happening all over again.

"Don't be a goober," Trinity chided her. "You just need to go out there and show everyone you can laugh at yourself, and it'll be no big deal."

She had a point. Nina had always been able to laugh at herself, and had never much cared what other people thought of her. So why did this feel so different, so humiliating? It was a totally new feeling, and Nina didn't like it.

Jordan poked her head over the half door. She had Freckles cross-tied in the aisle outside, where Trinity had been helping her paint his coat in Mardi Gras colors.

"I don't know, Trin," she said, her troubled hazel eyes darting from Trinity to Nina. "If I was Nina I wouldn't want to do the costume class either."

"But you're not her, and she's not you," Trinity

reminded her. She glanced at Nina. "Since when do you let something like this freak you out so much?"

"Since the entire world saw my lucky underwear," Nina retorted.

Trinity smirked. "The entire world already saw your underwear when I dared you to moon half of Bourbon Street that time," she pointed out. "So I mean, are you sure it's the world you're worried about? Or could it be a certain floppy-haired guy whose name rhymes with pet?"

"Huh?" Jordan blinked, looking confused.

Nina scowled at Trinity. "I don't know what you're talking about," she snapped. "Anyway, I'm starting to wonder if my gramma and uncle are right. Maybe Serena really is out to get me."

She was kidding—at least mostly—but Jordan's eyes went round and nervous. "Oh, you could totally be right!" she exclaimed. "See? I told you it was a bad idea!"

"Don't be a dork," Trinity told her. "Nina's too smart to believe in that stuff. Right, Neens?"

"Right." But secretly, Nina had to wonder: *What if?* Yes, she was smart—smart enough not to think she knew everything. Was there a chance, even a small one, that the legends about Serena could be real?

No, she told herself firmly, glancing at Jordan's pale, worried face. *I love Jordan, but I'm not going to let myself turn into her—or into Uncle Oscar or Gramma Rose, either.*

"You know, you're right," she told Trinity, dropping the brush into Breezy's grooming bucket. "I worked way too hard on that costume to back out now. No way am I missing that costume class." She patted Breezy's round rump. "I mean, I managed to mess us up enough so we only came in fifth in our division instead of getting the championship ribbon Breezy deserves. I've got to make it up to him somehow, right?"

"That's my girl!" Trinity cheered.

Jordan still looked dubious. "Are you sure?" she said. "I mean, if Serena really is out to get you . . ."

Hearing her say it out loud only reminded Nina how silly it was to believe in ghosts, even for a second. "I'm positive," she said firmly. "Now who wants to help me turn this adorable Chincoteague pony into a super-spooky steed?"

"Next, we have Nina Peralt on Bay Breeze," the announcer's voice rang out over the stable's PA system. "They're dressed as the ghost of Nina's many-times-great-aunt Serena, a native New Orleanian with a tragic past who lived during the Civil War, and her ghostly horse."

The audience applauded, and Nina heard a few whoops from her friends and relatives as she and Breezy cantered into the ring. Nina knew they looked great—Jordan and Trinity had helped her get ready, dusting Breezy's coat with talcum powder to make him look ghostly and weaving the ribbons and scraps of gray, white, and silver fabric Nina had brought into his mane and tail. Nina herself looked suitably spooky in her long, tattered gray tunic, pale gray gloves, and dark breeches. A wig she'd found at a junk shop was glued to her spare riding helmet, its lank gray locks streaming out behind her as she rode.

Nina circled the ring at a canter, enjoying the cheers of the crowd. Now that she was out here, she was glad she hadn't let what had happened earlier keep her from entering the costume class. This was fun!

Later, after all the riders had taken care of their mounts and returned to the ring on foot, the stable owner finally announced the winners of the costume prizes. Nina and Jordan ended up tied for first place in the local-interest category, while Nina also won second prize for spookiest, behind a pretty convincing Headless Horseman costume.

"Well done, baby," Aunt Toni said, touching the colorful ribbons fluttering on Nina's backpack. "You did good today."

"Thanks." Nina smiled, accepting congratulations from the rest of her family as well.

But she couldn't help feeling a little distracted. The day hadn't turned out quite as she'd been expecting. Normally that wouldn't bother her—Nina loved surprises. But today she couldn't seem to stop thinking about the things that had gone wrong. Like Breezy stopping at that fence in their first jumping class. Or the cat-and-mouse spook that had caused chaos for the entire ring. Or especially that horrible ripping sound as her breeches split down the middle . . .

Realizing that her mother was talking to her, she

blinked. "Uh, sorry," she said. "Spaced out there for a sec. What?"

"I said, are any of your friends coming to your dad's gig tonight?" her mother said.

Nina blinked again. She'd forgotten all about her father's show. Right then, the thought of spending that evening crammed into a dark, smoky jazz club didn't seem as appealing as it should have.

"No, I don't think so," she said, suddenly glad she'd forgotten to mention the gig to Jordan and Trin and the others. She glanced at her father. "Actually, would you be mad if I didn't make it? I kind of want to hang out with Breezy a little longer—you know, thank him for being such an awesome pony today."

Her father looked surprised, but he shrugged. "No worries, I get it," he said. "You go pamper that good pony of yours."

"Maybe you can come join up with us later," DeeDee suggested. "I'll leave my phone on vibrate so I'll catch it if you call or text, okay?"

"Sure, sounds good." But Nina had hardly taken in her

cousin's words. She'd just spotted Brett wandering in their direction. "Listen, break a leg, Dad, okay? Catch you guys at home." She sprinted off in the opposite direction from Brett before anyone else could say another word.

A couple of hours later, Cypress Trail Stables was quiet as Nina led Breezy out of the barn and down a gravel path lined with live oaks. It was after sunset, but between the city lights and the full moon rising over the skyline, Nina had no trouble seeing where she was going.

Soon they reached one of the small fenced paddocks where the stable's residents took turns stretching their legs and getting some fresh air. There was only a little bit of grass in there, but Breezy dove for it eagerly as soon as Nina let him.

"Eat up, babycakes," she said softly, smiling as his flexible lips wiggled around looking for the most succulent blades of grass. "You earned it today."

She perched on a rocky outcropping and watched her pony graze. Miss Adaline would have had a fit if she'd seen her—she was all about safety, and always warned her riders that sitting down near a horse was never a good idea—but Nina knew that the instructor had left half an hour ago. Besides, Nina was exhausted after the long day and wasn't sure she could stay on her feet any longer.

Staring at Breezy, she felt overwhelmed by pride tinged with regret. If only they'd done better in the show today! Nina knew he was the best pony ever, and she wished he'd had a chance to prove that in front of everyone.

Good thing ponies don't care about blue ribbons, she thought. *Or about super-embarrassing wardrobe malfunctions either.*

Once again she felt her cheeks go hot as she remembered that ripping sound as her breeches split. How was she ever going to live that down? It was bad enough that it had happened at all—why had it happened in front of Brett, of all people?

What difference should that make? she asked herself.

But there in the moonlight, with nobody else around, she had to admit that it *did* make a difference. She'd been looking at Brett in a new way lately, whether she wanted to accept it or not, and that was why she couldn't laugh off the incident like she normally would.

She grimaced, not sure she liked what that meant. *Okay, whatever,* she thought. *If this is romance, I should probably just stick to ponies!*

◆ CHAPTER ◆
7

NINA SPENT SUNDAY MORNING HELPING her mother pack up some photos and other stuff for her art-gallery show. After that she and her father made a big pot of gumbo for lunch, and then Nina played with the cats for a while.

Finally, though, she knew she couldn't put it off any longer—it was time to check in with the Pony Post and let them know what had happened.

When she signed on, there were a few messages from each of the other members asking how the show had gone. But none of the girls were live on the site at the moment.

Nina was glad. It would be easier to get the story out all at once, without having to stop and explain things along the way. She opened a text box and typed fast, pouring out the whole sordid tale—stops, spooks, splits, and all. Well, *almost* all. She didn't mention Brett, but she figured that was okay. She'd tell her friends about him whenever she figured out whether there was anything to tell.

Once she'd hit send, she actually felt a little better. Her Pony Post friends would understand how she was feeling, if anyone would.

After dinner, Nina checked in again and found responses from all three of the other Pony Posters.

[HALEY] O Nina! Sorry you had a rough time at yr show. But don't feel bad—u were prolly still miles better than me and Wings at our first event. We did rly well at the jumping stuff, but totally blew the dressage phase. I think we got the lowest score of the day other than the horse that jumped out of the ring and bucked off his rider on top of the judges' table! LOL!

[BROOKE] Yah, I was super nervous when Foxy and I did our camp show over the summer. Remember? All the other girls were super experienced at showing, and I was sure I'd make a fool of myself . . . I bet u did way better than u think! You won some ribbons, right?

[HALEY] Brooke's right—and u won two prizes for yr costume! That's awesome!!!!

[MADDIE] Sorry, late checking in—long soccer practice, ugh! But speaking of soccer: Nina, u could never possibly embarrass yrself as much as I do on a regular basis. I mean, did I tell you about the time I was so psyched up for a soccer championship game that I ran out of the locker room w/o remembering to put on my shorts??? talk about an embarrassing underwear moment!!

Nina found herself smiling as she read through her friends' comments, and she burst out laughing at Maddie's story. Was it true? She had no clue—with Maddie, it could go either way. But it didn't matter. It had made her laugh, which made her feel better.

"Thanks, guys," she murmured, scanning the rest of the Pony Posters' encouraging words. "You're the best!"

She typed a quick response and then signed off, feeling a little better—at least until she thought about Brett, and the expression on his face as he'd stared at her lucky underwear.

Oh well, she thought as she flopped onto her bed, too tired to bother pulling her bead drapes closed to dampen the moonlight shining in her window. *Silver lining? I won't have to face him first thing tomorrow morning, since he goes to a different school. I'll just have to do my best to avoid him until he forgets about what happened.* She grimaced. *That should only take, oh, about a million years. . . .*

Nina wasn't sure what time it was when she woke out of a restless sleep with her sheets tangled around her legs.

She sat up and pushed a sweaty strand of hair off her forehead, glancing out the window at the almost-full moon. For a second the window frame and the darkened shapes of her furniture looked odd and unfamiliar, as if she were expecting to be somewhere else entirely. . . .

She'd been dreaming; she knew that much. Dredging a few wisps of memory out of her fuzzy mind, she recalled running and running, crashing through sheets of Spanish moss and cobwebs but not daring to stop. Who or what had been chasing her?

Serena, she realized with a shiver.

Yes, she was pretty sure that was right—she'd known it was her ghostly ancestor, even though she'd never actually seen her. She hadn't *wanted* to see her, because she knew that if she did . . . something . . . what? What was she expecting to happen?

A yawn split her face, and more of the details of her dream slipped away. Still, Nina wasn't quite ready to lie down and close her eyes again. She stared at the moon, her tired mind producing an uneasy thought: *What if the stories are true?*

◆ ◆ ◆

By the time she pushed through the school's heavy front door on Monday morning, Nina had nearly forgotten about her dream and the midnight musings it had produced. She was focused on that day's math quiz, which she'd barely studied for over the weekend.

"Nina! You're here! I thought you'd be too embarrassed to show your face after what happened."

Nina glanced up. Her friend Keisha was standing in a doorway nearby, grinning at her, her brown eyes twinkling with mischief.

"Huh?" Nina said, still mostly thinking about the quiz.

"You know—*rrrip*?" Keisha's grin widened. "I mean, I thought it was bad when I put my shirt on backward after gym class and didn't notice for like half the day. But this takes the prize!"

Nina forced a smile in return. Keisha was a good friend, and Nina knew she was only teasing. Why shouldn't she? Normally Nina was first in line to make fun of herself when she did something embarrassing or boneheaded.

"Yeah, totally embarrassing." Nina wondered how

Keisha had heard about the incident, since she hadn't attended the show.

Then again, maybe she didn't need to wonder. Plenty of people had been there, including her friend Livi, an inveterate gossip. The news was probably all over school by now.

She forced a grin as Keisha ducked past her, obviously staring at her backside. "Don't worry—all clear," Keisha said. "Your pants are still in one piece." She grinned at Nina, clearly expecting a joking response in return.

"Thanks for checking," Nina said as lightly as she could. "But it's cool—I wore an extra pair of pants under these just in case."

Keisha laughed and raised her hand for a high five. "Wish I'd been at that show," she said. "It must've been hilarious. Too bad nobody got video!"

"Yeah." Nina swallowed a sigh, hoping this would blow over soon. "Too bad."

". . . so I spent all day yesterday dealing with everyone at school wanting to know if I was wearing my lucky underwear again," Nina said, jiggling Breezy's lead rope to stop him from eating a moldy-looking sandwich someone had left on the grass. It was Tuesday afternoon, and she and Jordan were grazing their ponies on the levee after their ride. Nina had been a little late arriving at the barn, since the streetcar she'd taken home from school had broken down and she'd had to walk an extra ten blocks. So this was her first chance to talk to Jordan aside from a few quick texts earlier in the day.

Jordan shot her a sympathetic look. "Totally embarrassing."

"I guess." Nina wiped her forehead, which was beaded with sweat. It was a hot, sticky afternoon, and the park was crowded with people trying to escape the sweltering city streets. "I mean, I can deal with being the butt of a joke for a day or two. The trouble is, it didn't end there."

"What do you mean?"

"Well, things were settling down by lunchtime yesterday," Nina said. "Then I went to the bathroom and had toilet paper stuck to my shoe when I came out." She grimaced at the memory. "I didn't notice for like an hour, until someone finally told me."

Jordan winced. "Oh, wow. That stinks." She giggled. "Um, no pun intended?"

"Ha-ha," Nina said heavily. She stared at Breezy, who hadn't lifted his head from the grass since they'd arrived. "So then yesterday after school I was really feeling the need for some relaxing Breezy time to take my mind off it all. But when I got to the barn, he'd managed to cut his nose in the stall somehow."

"Really? Where?" Jordan dragged her horse closer, peering at Nina's pony's nose. "Oh yeah, I see it! Did he need stitches?"

"No, he's fine, thank goodness. One of the grooms put some goop on it and that stopped the bleeding." Nina shook her head. "But I was still kind of worried about him this morning and ended up spacing out during social studies and totally blowing my oral report."

"Yikes!" Jordan said. "That's not like you. You're usually, like, a superstar at stuff like that."

"I know." Nina shook her head, wondering if her social studies teacher would let her redo the report. "It's starting to feel like I'm cursed this week or something."

"Cursed?" Jordan said quickly. "Wait, does that mean you're ready to admit you might have messed with the wrong ghost?"

"Don't be ridiculous," Nina said, though her words came out sounding limp and unconvincing even to her.

Jordan put her hands on her hips. "Come on. You can't tell me it's not weird timing. First the stuff at the show, then the rest right after that . . . What if Serena's punishing you for dressing up as her? Or just for being, you know, happy and awesome and stuff, like you said she's done to people in your family before?"

"Some people think she's done that," Nina mumbled. "Not me." But once again her words didn't sound very certain.

She heard someone calling her name and Jordan's. Her heart skipped a beat as she realized it was Brett. He was jogging toward them across the grass.

Oh no, Nina thought. *This is so not what I need right now.*

By the time the thought finished crossing her mind, Brett had reached them. "Hey," he said breathlessly, grinning at Nina. "I've been looking all over for you! Uh, not you, Nina—I mean, why would I be looking for you, right?" He laughed. "I was looking for my sister."

"Huh? Why, what do you want?" Jordan didn't seem very interested in her brother's arrival. She was still watching Nina with a troubled look on her face.

"I figured you probably forgot Mom wants you home early for dinner tonight because of her meeting. So I'm reminding you." Brett took a step closer to Nina and Breezy. "Hey, runt pony, how's it going?"

Breezy finally lifted his head from the grass as Brett approached. At the same moment, Nina took a quick step back out of Brett's way. As she did, she felt her elbow connect—hard—with the pony's injured nose.

"Oh, Breezy, I'm sorry!" she blurted out as the pony jerked his head back, yanking the lead rope out of her hand.

"Whoa, loose horse!" Brett exclaimed, leaping forward. "I'll get him."

Breezy had already stopped. But at Brett's sudden movement, the pony jumped back again.

"Stop right there, horse!" Brett yelled, grabbing for the dangling lead line.

"Wait!" Nina cried. "If you just let me—"

It was too late. Startled by Brett's sudden move, Breezy let out a snort of alarm and wheeled around, taking off across the grass at a canter.

"Breezy, stop! Whoa, boy!" Nina called, running after him.

Brett caught up to her quickly. "Should I try to head him off?" he asked breathlessly.

"No!" Nina snapped. "You've done enough."

Brett didn't seem to hear her. He was already veering to the side, clearly trying to angle across in front of the pony.

Meanwhile Breezy had slowed to a brisk trot and was heading toward a group of young men hanging out around a boom box. They saw him coming and jumped to their feet, hollering and whooping. Breezy skidded to a stop, then spun and cantered off toward the river.

"Breezy! Easy, boy!" Nina called.

She winced as she saw that the pony was now heading

toward two women, one young and solidly built, the other a frail older lady with a walker. The younger woman saw the pony and let out a shout, jumping forward and waving her arms over her head to shoo Breezy away. The pony turned, now trotting off in the direction of a family having a picnic. The father leaped to his feet.

"Hey, your horse is loose!" he cried. "Here—I'll get him."

He lunged forward, but Breezy was faster, spinning away before the man could grab the rope. Soon the pony was cantering off along the path in the opposite direction.

The next few minutes were like a nightmare for Nina. More people saw what was happening and rushed over to try to help, which only got Breezy even more riled up. The normally lazy pony dodged and wheeled, ducking every well-meaning person who tried to grab him. It was only when Jordan finally caught up, Freckles trailing along behind her, that Nina was able to grab her pony when he trotted toward his stablemate.

"Got him!" Nina gasped out, clutching the lead rope. She was shaking so hard she was afraid she'd drop it.

"Show's over," Brett called to the people gathering around. "Thanks for the help, everyone."

Nina gritted her teeth. The bystanders hadn't been much help at all—and neither had Brett, for that matter. But she knew it wasn't their fault. Most people didn't know how to act around horses. How many times had Miss Adaline reminded her students of that before they set off for a ride through Audubon Park?

"Is Breezy okay?" Jordan asked. "He looks pretty hot."

Nina nodded. Her pony's flanks were heaving, and his head was hanging low. Every inch of his pinto coat seemed to be coated with sweat.

"Yeah." Nina tried not to look at Brett, who was watching her—probably thinking what a huge dork she was, Nina figured. "I'd better get him back to the stable and hose him off."

◆ CHAPTER ◆

8

[MADDIE] Happy Wednesday, everyone!

[HALEY] Hey, M—I'm here too.

[MADDIE] Cool! Hey, did u see Nina's post from yesterday? Nina, sounds terrifying! I don't know what I'd do if Cloudy got loose from me in the middle of a big city!!! I'm totally picturing her galloping thru San Fran as I type this, ugh!

[HALEY] I know what I'd do if it happened to me & Wings—prolly faint on the spot, lol!

Srsly, tho, Nina, I'm sorry too! Glad B was OK, tho.

[MADDIE] Yah, me too. But listen, u don't rly think Serena has anything to do w/all the bad stuff that's been happening, do you?

[HALEY] No way, Nina was just kidding about that. She doesn't believe in that stuff.

[MADDIE] Well, neither do I, but my dad and I watched this old spy movie last night on TV—part of it was set in New Orleans, and there was a bunch of voodoo stuff. It reminded me of what your fam told u about Serena and voodoo and all that.

[HALEY] What r u saying? That Nina's under some voodoo curse? Ya, right!!

[MADDIE] LOL, I'm just saying u never

know. Oops, Mom's calling me—gtg.

Will check in later. Hang in there, Nina!

[BROOKE] Hello? Anyone still here?

[BROOKE] Oh well, guess not. Hi Nina—sounds

like a scary time yesterday! Glad Breezy

cooled out OK after all that running around.

[BROOKE] Btw, meant to tell u—I found

this cool genealogy site online over the

w/e. If u want, I could research Serena

and see if she and her story are even real.

Maybe that would make u feel better?

[BROOKE] Anyway, let me know!

Nina smiled as she read over her friends' comments on
her cell phone. It was late Wednesday evening, and she was

sitting on the wooden floorboards of her cousin Kim's dance studio. Kim was busy with some paperwork in her office, and none of the other dancers had turned up yet. Nina knew she should spend the extra time stretching and practicing, but she hadn't been able to resist checking in on the Pony Post first. She'd been so busy all day she hadn't had a chance to log on since updating her friends the evening before. But typing on the phone's tiny keyboard was a hassle, so after scanning their messages a second time, she signed off with a mental note to respond when she got home.

Glad I filled them in last night, she thought as she tucked her phone into her bag and started her pre-dance stretches. *They always make me feel better about everything. And hey, maybe I'll tell Brooke to go for it with the genealogy stuff. It would be fun to learn more about the real Serena— even if I know she's got nothing to do with my bad luck lately.*

As she bent her left elbow toward her right knee to stretch out her back, the door swung open, and two of the other dancers in her class hurried in. Both were a year older than Nina. One of them, a tall, willowy blonde named Ivy, lived just a block away from Nina's house.

"Hey, Nina," Ivy said, dropping her bag beside Nina's. "I hear you've been having a bad week."

Nina's head snapped up. "Where'd you hear that?"

"You know Brett, right?" Ivy kicked off her shoes, then peeled off her jeans, revealing tights and a leotard beneath.

"Yeah." Nina tried to keep her voice sounding normal. "I know him."

Ivy nodded. "He told me your horse freaked out at some show over the weekend, and again the other day at the park," she said. "He said something about you bombing some school project, too."

"Sounds like the worst week ever," the other girl put in, not looking up as she dug through her bag. "Bummer, Nina."

Nina didn't respond. She couldn't believe Brett was telling everyone about all her problems! How did he even know about that oral report, anyway?

Jordan, she realized. She told her mother about everything that worried her or made her nervous, and Nina supposed her problems qualified—especially since Jordan still seemed convinced that Serena's vengeful ghost was behind all the trouble. Of course, Jordan was always saying that Brett never listened to anything she said, but he seemed to have made an exception for embarrassing stories about Nina.

Ivy dropped to the floor and stretched to touch her toes. "I had a week like that once," she said, her voice slightly muffled by her own legs. "First I got a bad haircut when my stylist spaced out while she was working, then I flunked a big test, and I was so freaked out about it that I ended up getting in a huge fight with my sister, and . . ."

While she was talking, several other dancers wandered in and took their places. Most of them listened curiously to what Ivy was saying, and before Nina could say a word, Ivy was filling them in on Nina's problems.

"Wow, that's crazy, Nina," one of the girls said as she stretched. "You usually have super good luck, but maybe that's changing."

"What do you mean?" Nina asked.

The girl shrugged. "I mean you have a really cool life, right? Cool parents, a cool cousin who teaches dance—"

"Your own pony," another girl put in with a laugh. "I mean, how many people in New Orleans can say that?"

Nina supposed they had a point. Had she led a charmed life until now? Could that have attracted Serena's attention—and had she decided to make Nina pay?

Don't be ridiculous, she told herself. *There's no such thing as ghosts. Especially not envious ghosts who don't want people to be happy. I mean, how ridiculous is it that I'm even thinking about this?*

"Okay, people!" Her cousin Kim strode into the studio and clapped her hands. "Everyone here? Good—let's get started. At the barre, please, girls."

Nina hopped to her feet with everyone else and took her place between Ivy and a petite younger girl named Beth at the long wooden barre in front of the mirror. She took a few deep breaths, hoping she'd stretched enough.

Kim didn't waste any time getting started, running the dancers through a few warm-up exercises at the barre. Normally, dance class, like riding, was a place where Nina forgot everything else in her life, good or bad. Tonight, however, she felt distracted. The moon was rising, gleaming in through the plate glass window at one end of the studio. The big mirror covering the opposite wall reflected its pale light, making everything look a little spooky and unreal. Every time she caught a glimpse of the moon, Nina got the feeling it was a huge eye watching her.

Snap out of it, girl, Nina told herself the first time she missed a step. *You're freaking yourself out for no reason.*

But a few minutes later her gaze slipped to the moon again. A little hint of last night's dreams floated through her mind, making her wonder . . .

At that moment the rest of the class took a sideways step, startling Nina out of her thoughts. She quickly jumped sideways, trying to catch up, but she moved too fast and stumbled. Before she could catch her balance, she crashed into the dancer beside her.

"Ow!" Beth cried, hopping on one foot. "That was my toe!"

"Sorry," Nina blurted out. "Um, I lost my balance for a sec. Are you okay?"

"Yeah, I guess." Beth shot her a disgruntled look as she shook out her foot and got back in position—a little farther away from Nina than before.

Cousin Kim was watching. "You okay, Nina?"

Nina nodded, taking a deep breath and adjusting herself back into position. "It won't happen again."

It didn't. Nina managed to keep her focus enough not to mess up for the rest of the class, though her gaze still slipped to the watchful moon once in a while. The class seemed to drag on forever, but finally Kim called for a stop.

"That's enough for tonight, girls," she said. "See you all next week."

Ten minutes later, the last of the other dancers finished packing up and headed out, leaving Nina alone with her cousin. Kim always drove Nina home after class, since it ended late and the studio wasn't in the best neighborhood. She liked to joke that it was mostly because she liked having Nina stick around to help her tidy up the place after a long day of classes. But Nina was pretty sure it also had something to do with the fact that her cousin had a standing invitation to stay for dinner at her place. Kim was single, and her tiny apartment at the edge of the French Quarter had a cramped, outdated kitchen with a half-size refrigerator and virtually no counter space, which made it hard to do much more than heat frozen dinners in the microwave.

"Can you run the broom over the floor, Nina?" Kim said. "I've got to check on something in the office—back in a sec."

"Sure." Nina grabbed the broom and got to work.

As she swept, she found herself drifting toward the window. When she reached it, she stopped, staring up at the moon, which was high in the sky by now. She was still standing there when Kim returned a few minutes later.

"Something going on outside?" Kim asked.

Nina jumped, startled. "Oh! Sorry, just got distracted," she said, quickly resuming her sweeping. "The moon's really bright tonight."

Kim glanced at the moon, then at Nina. "I suppose so. Are you okay today, Nina? You seemed kind of out of it during class."

Nina should have guessed her cousin would notice. Kim was like that—not only could she pinpoint exactly which limb was slightly off in a dancer's position, but she could always tell when someone was in a funky mood or feeling not quite right.

"Actually, it's been a bizarre week," Nina said. "All sorts of things have been going wrong or weird or just, you know, not quite normal. Starting with the horse show last weekend." She shot her cousin a sidelong look. "I'm starting to think Great-Aunt Serena is after me."

She'd meant the comment to sound like a joke, but it hadn't quite come out that way. Kim raised an eyebrow.

"Okay, Gramma Rose," she quipped. Then she peered at Nina. "You're not serious, are you?"

"No," Nina said quickly. Then she shrugged. "Not really. I mean, I don't know. It just seems like everything started going wacko when I dressed up as Serena. And Jordan—"

Kim rolled her eyes. "Yeah, Jordan, I know. That girl's scared of her own shadow—you probably never should've told her about Serena if you didn't want to hear about it ever after." She smiled. "But listen, Nina, you can't let Jittery Jordan rub off on you. Uncle Oscar or Gramma, either. Serena was just a sad, lonely woman who never got over the tragedy in her life. That doesn't mean she's still hanging around, haunting our family."

"I know, I know," Nina said. "I don't believe in ghosts, okay? You know that. It's just . . ." Her voice trailed off into a sigh. "I don't know. It's a little weird, you know?"

Kim looked dubious. "Okay. But I think you know as well as I do that Serena hasn't budged from her grave in St. Louis Cemetery since the day she was buried there in the year eighteen-whatever."

"St. Louis Cemetery? Really, that's where she's buried? You mean the famous one?" Nina knew there were actually three cemeteries by that name in New Orleans. But most people thought first of the one known as St. Louis No. 1, near the French Quarter. Lots of tourists went there to see the graves of famous New Orleanians, like the first African-American mayor and Marie Laveau, the famous voodoo priestess.

"That's the one. I've never seen Serena's grave myself, but I remember your dad and Johnny talking about trying to find it and spending the night there on a dare when we were kids."

"Did they ever do it?" Nina had trouble imagining her responsible attorney father sneaking into the fenced cemetery after hours. Then again, based on the tales the family told over their weekly dinners, Gabe Peralt and his nephew and best friend John had gotten into all sorts of mischief as teens.

Kim shook her head. "I'm not sure," she said. "I was away at ballet camp most of that summer, so if they did do it, I probably wouldn't have heard about it." She winked. "Especially after the way I tattled on them when they used Ma's best colander to collect worms for fishing."

Nina smiled, though she wasn't really thinking about the worm incident, a favorite story among the entire family. "I can't believe I didn't know Serena was buried in St. Louis Cemetery, with all those famous people," she said. "That's pretty cool."

Or it would be, anyway, she thought, her gaze sneaking back to the moon, *if not for the fact that Serena's ghost seems to be haunting me. . . .*

◆ CHAPTER ◆
9

"THIS IS NICE, ISN'T IT?" NINA SAID, SETTLING back in the saddle. "It seems like forever since we just took a nice, easy trail ride."

"Yeah." Jordan was riding beside her on the wide, well-groomed park trail. "We've been awfully busy lately getting ready for the show. It feels good to just ride for a change—you know, without worrying about whether my heels are down enough or if Freckie's using his hind end properly or whatever."

Nina nodded, closing her eyes for a second to enjoy the feel of the breeze on her face. The weather had finally cooled down a little, and it was pleasant in the shade of the live oaks lining the path.

"The show was fun," she said after a moment. "But I think this is my favorite part of riding. Just hanging out exploring the world with my pony. Know what I mean?"

"Sure." Jordan shrugged. "Only I'm not sure the show was even that much fun. It was a lot of stress."

Nina opened her eyes and glanced over at her friend. "But you did great—you and Freckie were third in our whole division!"

"Only because Freckie's a superstar." Jordan gave her horse a pat. "Seriously, I was just hanging on for the ride. He did all the work."

Nina knew that wasn't true. Yes, Freckles was a terrific, well-trained horse. Maybe he was even smart and experienced enough to listen to the announcer during the flat class and change gaits as commanded. But even Freckles couldn't read a course map and then steer his way through the jumps in the right order!

She didn't bother to point that out, though. Jordan wouldn't pay any attention anyway.

"So listen," Nina said instead. "I found out something interesting yesterday from Kim. It's about Serena."

"Really? I thought Kim was way too practical to believe in Serena," Jordan said.

Nina laughed. "What do you mean? She has no choice to believe in her—everyone agrees Serena was a real person."

"Okay, you know what I mean." Jordan smiled. "She doesn't believe in the haunting stuff and all the rest."

Nina didn't respond to that. "Anyway, now I guess I can prove she was real in case anybody has any doubts," she said. "Because Kim says Serena's buried in St. Louis Cemetery."

Jordan glanced over, looking surprised. "You mean *the* St. Louis Cemetery?"

"Uh-huh." Nina nudged Breezy with one heel to steer him around a fallen tree branch on the trail. "Isn't that cool?"

"Yeah." But Jordan wasn't paying much attention anymore. She was peering ahead, her expression concerned.

Nina looked that way too. They were approaching an open grassy area. Half a dozen little kids were shrieking and running around. Nina saw a ball fly out and across the path, with all the kids in hot pursuit.

"Looks like a game of keep-away or something," she commented.

Jordan looked tense. "Do you think Freckles will spook if that ball comes too close?" she said. "Maybe we should turn around and go back the other way."

For a second the image of Breezy spooking at that cat and mouse flitted through Nina's mind. But she immediately banished the thought. That had been a once-in-a-lifetime thing—the extra excitement of the show combined with bad luck.

"Don't be ridic," she told Jordan lightly. "Neither of these guys is going to bat an eye at something like that. They're city ponies, remember?"

"I guess you're right." Jordan still looked nervous, but she took a deep breath and kept her horse at Breezy's side as the two equines walked on.

When the girls reached the lawn, the kids were

halfway across squabbling over something. None of them even glanced at the horses.

"Good," Jordan muttered. "Let's get through here before they come back this way."

"Chill out," Nina said with a laugh. "They could bounce that ball off Freckie's head and he still wouldn't—"

Before she could finish, one of the kids let out a shout. There was the sound of a foot connecting solidly with rubber, and a moment later the ball came flying toward them.

Nina tensed, waiting for Breezy to spook as he'd done at the show. But all her pony did was glance at the ball as he ambled on.

Whew! Nina relaxed, smiling at her own reaction. *See? I was right—it was just the crazy show atmosphere making Breezy edgy before. Now he's back to being his normal, perfect self.*

She leaned forward to give him a pat. Meanwhile one of the little kids was racing over to retrieve the ball, chased by one of his friends.

"I'll get it!" the first kid yelled.

"No, me!" the second cried, spurting past the first and kicking it before his friend got there.

"Hey, careful!" Jordan exclaimed as the ball rolled toward the horses.

It bounced off Freckles's leg; he jumped but then stayed still. Then the ball rolled under Breezy's right forefoot just as he was taking a step.

"Watch it, Breeze-man," Nina exclaimed as her pony stumbled.

Breezy tried to catch himself, but the ball shot out and hit his other foreleg, causing him to stumble again—and this time land heavily on his knees. Nina was tossed forward onto his withers, where she scrabbled to hold on to his mane and neck. But it was no use—as her pony struggled to regain his feet, she felt herself slipping sideways. . . .

"Oof!" she grunted as she hit the ground, landing on her hip and one arm.

"Nina!" Jordan yelped. "Oh my gosh, are you okay? Nina?"

"I'm fine," Nina gasped, the wind knocked out of her by the fall. She rolled aside as Breezy finally managed to scramble back to his feet. He stood there, breathing hard and looking confused.

The little kids had already grabbed their ball and run away without a backward glance. Nina glared after them as she climbed to her feet and grabbed Breezy's dangling reins.

"Are you hurt?" Jordan sounded almost hysterical. "Should I call nine-one-one?"

Nina glanced over, realizing that her friend had her cell phone in her hand with one shaky finger hovering over the keypad. "No!" she said. "I'm totally fine. I didn't even hit my head." She touched her riding helmet, then brushed some dirt off her pants. "It's no big deal."

It wasn't—at least that was what Nina was trying to tell herself. She was fine, and so was Breezy. And it wasn't as if she'd never fallen off before. When she'd first learned to ride, she used to joke she spent more time on the ground than in the saddle. That was a slight exaggeration, of course—thanks to her years of dance training, Nina had excellent balance. But those years of dance had also taught her to be physically fearless when trying new things, and she'd come off often enough to get over any fear of falling she might have had.

But this was different. *Breezy never stumbles*, she

thought uneasily. *Isn't it kind of strange that he did—just when I was thinking how perfect he was? Just when I was convincing myself that the whole Serena thing was a figment of my imagination?*

"Do you want me to call the stable?" Jordan still had her phone in her hand. "Or should I get off and hold him while you catch your breath?"

"No, I'm good." Nina checked her girth, then walked Breezy a few steps to make sure he really was okay. He seemed fine, so she swung back into the saddle. She forced a smile as she glanced over at Jordan. "I'll just tell Great-Aunt Serena not to let it happen again," she quipped.

Jordan gasped. "Do you think Serena had something to do with this?" She didn't give Nina a chance to respond. "Of course she did! Duh, I totally should've realized it myself. Oh, Nina—this is getting really scary now! What are you going to do?"

"Do?" Nina gave Breezy a nudge to start him walking. "I'm going to finish this trail ride, that's what I'm going to do."

"No, I'm serious!" Jordan urged her horse forward to

catch up. "You have to do something about this Serena situation before it gets even worse. I mean, you could be in danger, you know?"

Nina rolled her eyes, trying not to shiver at her friend's words. "What am I supposed to do? Call someone in to do an exorcism?"

"Maybe," Jordan replied seriously. "Or maybe you need to look into this whole voodoo thing, you know? Maybe there's someone who could help you, like, banish Serena's evil spirit or something."

Nina rolled her eyes again. "Please."

"No, listen, this could seriously work." Jordan stared at her. "If voodoo is what's giving Serena the power to hurt you, maybe you need to fight fire with fire!"

"Let's not get crazy here," Nina said firmly. "I'm not hurt, okay? And I'm pretty sure the whole Serena thing is all in my head."

Jordan cocked her head. "*Pretty* sure?"

"Totally sure," Nina corrected. "Anyway, like I was saying, I just found out she's buried in St. Louis Cemetery. I think I'll go there and see her grave—maybe talk to her a little, apologize for using her life for a silly costume." She smiled. "Put my mind at ease. Psychology, not voodoo, you know?"

Jordan looked unconvinced. "I guess it's worth a try. Do you want me to come with?"

"Sure, that would be great," Nina said. "I might not believe in ghosts, but it's still kind of creepy being in a cemetery all alone."

"Not that you're likely to be alone at St. Louis," Jordan pointed out. "You'll probably be fighting hordes of tourists to get to Serena's grave."

Nina laughed. "True. Come on, let's get these guys back to the barn, and we'll head up there right away."

Twenty minutes later, Breezy and Freckles were back in their stalls eating hay and the two girls were heading for the exit. On the way, they passed one of the grooms. He called out a greeting.

"Where are you two off to?" he asked with a grin. "Looks like you're in a hurry."

"St. Louis Cemetery," Nina replied. "We, uh, want to check it out. Um, school project?"

The groom glanced at his watch. "Hope it's not due tomorrow," he said. "Because St. Louis closes at three, and it's past four thirty now."

"What?" Nina traded a glance with Jordan. "Are you sure?"

"Positive. My brother used to be a tour guide there."

"Oh." Nina's shoulders slumped. "Okay, thanks. You just saved us a trip."

As the groom hurried off, Jordan stared at Nina. "The voodoo shops stay open late," she said. "And I know one we could try—it's a real one, not one of the junky tourist traps. We could go over there right now."

"That's okay," Nina said with a smile. "We'll just hit up the cemetery right after school tomorrow."

"See anything?" Jordan asked.

Nina was peering at yet another half-illegible slab of stone. "Not yet," she said, straightening up. "I can't really read this one, but the date of birth definitely doesn't match."

She looked around. It was Friday afternoon, and she

and Jordan were deep in St. Louis Cemetery, surrounded by a maze of crypts and mausoleums. In New Orleans the water table was very high, which meant most burials were aboveground. St. Louis Cemetery looked more like a miniature city of marble and stone than a regular burial ground.

The two girls had come straight there from their respective schools, but that didn't leave them much time to search for Serena's name. It was almost three o'clock, and most of the tourist groups that had been there when the girls arrived had already disappeared.

"I should've asked Dad if he knew exactly where Serena's grave is," Nina muttered as she hurried to the next crypt in line, a modest stone square discolored by moss. "Searching this place could take all night."

Jordan heard her and glanced over. "Don't even think about it," she said. "I am so not staying here after dark!"

"I know, I was only kidding," Nina assured her. She sighed and glanced around again. "I just wish we knew where to look."

She noticed a man walking down the path nearby.

He'd passed them earlier at the head of a large group of tourists.

"Hey, excuse me," Nina called out, hurrying toward him. "Are you a tour guide?"

The man peered at her over the tops of his spectacles. "Yes, I am," he said. "But I've just finished the last tour of the day. The cemetery is closing momentarily."

"I know." Nina shot him her most winning smile. "I just have a quick question, if that's okay?"

The man shrugged. "Sure, shoot."

"Someone told me I have a relative buried here," Nina said. "Her name was Serena Peralt, and she lived around the time of the Civil War. Do you happen to know where her grave is?"

"Serena Peralt?" The tour guide rubbed his chin thoughtfully. "Can't say I recall seeing that name here. Are you sure it's this St. Louis Cemetery? There are two others."

"Yes, thanks, I know." Nina bit her lip. "I'm pretty sure it's this one. Are you positive you haven't seen that name?"

"Sorry," the man replied. "I've been giving tours of this place for ten years, and I know just about every name in here by now. That one doesn't ring a bell."

"Okay, thanks anyway." Nina watched the man hurry off toward the exit.

Jordan joined her. "So now what?"

"I don't know." Nina sighed. "Kim was positive that Serena was in this St. Louis Cemetery. But she said she hadn't seen the grave herself—maybe she's wrong and it's one of the others after all. I can ask my dad if he knows."

"Okay," Jordan said. "But listen, in the meantime we're pretty close to that voodoo shop I was telling you about yesterday. Want to check it out? You know . . . just in case?"

"Just in case what?" Nina said. "Just in case I actually start believing in voodoo?"

"Come on," Jordan wheedled. "If you don't believe in it, then what can it hurt? We can just talk to the owner of the shop—see what she thinks. My neighbor says she's the real deal. Not just someone trying to make a buck off the tourists, but a genuine voodoo priestess, you know?"

Nina couldn't help being intrigued by the thought of

meeting a real voodoo priestess—even if she didn't actually believe in voodoo. Besides, Jordan had been super supportive of her problems, and Nina felt bad for continuing to poo-poo her help.

"What the heck," she said with a smile. "Like you said, it's worth a try. Lead the way to the voodoo shop."

A few minutes later they were pushing open the rattling front door of a tiny storefront a couple of blocks outside the French Quarter. The street was dusty and all but abandoned, populated with narrow, shabby shotgun houses and a liquor store and a convenience shop on the corner.

"Nice neighborhood," Nina said with a snort. "I can't believe the tourists don't come here."

"If they knew about this place, they would," Jordan said. "I told you, the woman who owns it is the real thing."

Nina didn't respond as she followed Jordan into the shop, which smelled of herbs and mildew. The place was just as narrow as every other building on the block, but the ceilings were high, and the packed shelves lining both walls gave the shop a claustrophobic feel. Nina glanced at the nearest shelf and saw books, candles, voodoo dolls, jars of herbs, and various other items she couldn't identify.

The woman behind the counter glanced up when the girls entered. She was tall and very thin, with high cheekbones, wide-set eyes, and dark skin. Her angular frame was wrapped in a multicolored shawl with a long fringe.

"Welcome," she said in a deep, sonorous voice with a faint West Indian lilt. "I am Madame Marceline, the proprietor of this shop. How may I assist you young ladies this fine day?"

Nina opened her mouth, ready to tell the woman they were just browsing. But Jordan stepped forward. "Actually," she said before Nina could speak, "we're looking for information about voodoo, because my friend here thinks her ancestor might be haunting her. . . ."

She went on to tell the woman all about Serena. After a while Nina shrugged and joined in, curious to hear what Madame Marceline might say about the old family legend. If nothing else, it would make a fun story to tell at that night's family dinner.

When they finished, Madame Marceline nodded slowly, looking thoughtful. "Fascinating," she said, staring at Nina. "It's always enlightening to meet someone with such deep roots in this city. Such deep, interesting roots. So you think this Serena is fixated on you and causing your recent problems, hmm?"

"Well . . ." Nina hesitated, not wanting to lie and say she believed—especially if Madame Marceline herself truly believed in ghosts and voodoo and all the rest. It seemed disrespectful somehow.

Luckily, the woman didn't wait for a response before continuing. "As I see it, you have two options," she said. "You could of course use evil voodoo to forcibly banish Serena's spirit back to the netherworld. However, since she is your ancestor, you might not wish to use a dark spell on her, in which case you can try to mollify her spirit using the properties of good voodoo."

Nina didn't believe in either kind of voodoo, but she could tell the woman was waiting for a response. "Good voodoo would be better, I guess," she told her.

"Yes, I thought you might feel that way." Madame Marceline stepped over to one of the shelves behind the counter and grabbed something. "In any case, this voodoo doll should take care of it either way. I'll also include a pamphlet with clear instructions for both options, all right? That way, if the good voodoo doesn't work . . ." She let the comment trail off with a rather ominous grimace.

"Um, thanks." Nina accepted the doll and pamphlet, realizing she couldn't back out now. She shot Jordan an annoyed look when Madame Marceline turned away to ring up the sale. This was definitely not how she'd planned to spend that week's allowance.

Soon she was stepping out of the shop with a small paper bag containing her new voodoo doll and everything she needed to use it. She took a deep breath of the city air, which smelled downright refreshing after the thick atmosphere of the voodoo shop.

"There," Jordan said as the door swung shut behind them. "Now at least you have something to try, right?"

"Don't be a goof," Nina said. "I was just being polite

back there. I'm not actually going to try to use voodoo to, like, banish Serena's spirit or whatever."

Jordan looked disappointed. "Are you sure? Madame Marceline made it sound like it would definitely work."

"Yeah—*if* the ghost of Serena was real. Which she isn't." Still, Nina couldn't help a slight shiver as she glanced over her shoulder at the voodoo shop.

None of this is for real, she told herself. *Is it?*

✦ CHAPTER ✦
10

AFTER TAKING THE STREETCAR BACK TO
their neighborhood, Nina and Jordan walked together as
far as Coliseum Street, where they usually parted ways to
head to their separate homes several blocks apart. When
they reached the corner, Jordan glanced at the bag in
Nina's hand.

"Seriously, Nina," she said. "Just think about it, okay?
Like I said, if you don't believe anyway, what can it hurt
to give it a try?" She paused. "Although it probably works
better if you can get yourself to believe at least a little. . . ."

"Whatever," Nina said. "I'll think about it, okay? See
you at the barn tomorrow."

"Yeah," Jordan said. "I'll be there by like four thirty. Do you think you'll be done at your mom's art show by then?"

Nina nodded. "Definitely. It starts at noon, and she doesn't expect me to hang around all day or anything. See you at four thirty."

As she walked the rest of the way home, the bag felt heavy in her hand. Should she follow Jordan's advice and try what Madame Marceline had told her to do? If nothing else, it might get Jordan to stop bugging her. . . .

When she stepped into her house, her parents were busy cooking oysters to bring along to that evening's family dinner at Aunt Vi's place. Bastet and Teniers were circling their feet, occasionally letting out a plaintive yowl at the scent of seafood floating through the air.

Nina smiled at the homey family scene, which made the whole idea of ghosts and voodoo seem even more ridiculous than it had before. "Need any help?" she asked.

Her mother glanced at her. "Oh good, you're home," she said. "We were about to send out a search party."

"Or at least a sternly worded text," Nina's father added

with a smile. "Just go get cleaned up and changed—we'll be ready to leave in twenty minutes or so."

Nina nodded and hurried down the hall to her room. Once she got there, she glanced at the paper bag in her hand, suddenly feeling foolish for even considering that a voodoo doll could solve her problems. She tossed the bag in a drawer, then kicked off her shoes.

Moments later, she'd finished washing her face and hands and changing into shorts and a T-shirt. She dropped her school clothes into the hamper in the bathroom and returned to her room, grabbing her laptop off the desk.

Soon she was logged into the Pony Post and scanning the latest entries. Haley had written something about her pony's latest cross-country jump school over some new obstacles she and her uncle and cousins had built in one of the cow fields, while Maddie had posted a couple of new photos of herself and Cloudy. Nina smiled, peering at a shot of Maddie mugging for the camera as she hugged the palomino pinto mare around the neck. Then she opened a new text box.

[NINA] Mads, u and C look adorable as always! And Haley, congrats on getting the new jumps built before winter. I hope u can still find them once there's twelve feet of snow on the ground, lol.

She posted that, then opened another box.

[NINA] But enough about you guys, lol.
I'm sure you're dying to hear the latest in the saga of the haunted pony girl . . .

She went on to fill them in on everything that had happened since her last entry, including her fall and the visit to the voodoo shop. She finished with a joking comment about trying the voodoo doll "by the light of the full moon this midnight."

Once her message posted, she clicked off the site and glanced at the clock. Her parents would be ready to leave soon. Did she have time to start her homework first? The weekend would be awfully busy between her mom's art-show opening and her planned barn time. . . .

As she was thinking about it, her cell phone rang. Nina's eyes widened when she saw the name on the readout.

"Brooke?" she exclaimed, pressing the phone to her ear. "Is that really you?"

"It's me." Brooke's voice sounded distant but familiar, even though they'd only spoken on the phone maybe a dozen times ever. "Hi, Nina."

"Hi!" Nina's face stretched into a grin. "I was just posting on the site."

"I know, I was just logging on when your message came up," Brooke said. "That's why I called. But listen, you still have unlimited long distance on your phone, right?"

"Right." Nina understood immediately. Brooke didn't even have her own cell phone yet—her parents were old-fashioned like that. And she'd mentioned before that the family didn't have a very good long-distance plan on their home phone, since they didn't have many faraway relatives and her father made all his business calls from work. "I'll call you right back," Nina added.

She hung up and hit Brooke's number, and soon the two of them were connected again. "So anyway," Brooke said, "I was going to put all this on the Pony Post, but I thought it might be quicker just to tell you. I've been looking into your dad's family tree like I said I would."

"Cool!" Nina said, flopping onto her bed and leaning back against her pillows. "Find anything good?"

"Well, I did find out that Serena was a real person," Brooke said. "And you're directly descended from her through your dad and granddad and their ancestors."

Nina nodded. She'd already known all that. "Thanks for looking into it," she said, a little disappointed. Since Brooke had gone to all the trouble to call, she'd been expecting something a little more exciting.

"You're welcome." Brooke hesitated. "But actually, that's not really why I called. Um, I read what you just posted—you know, about the voodoo stuff?"

"I was kidding," Nina said. "Don't worry, I haven't gone totally nutso."

"Good." Brooke sounded relieved. "Because there's really no evidence that Serena's ghost is haunting you, you know. And you're not usually the type of person to believe in stuff like that."

For a second, Nina felt annoyed. It was easy for Brooke to say there was no evidence—she was way up there safe and sound in Maryland, while Nina was the one dealing with Serena!

"But I know how easy it is to start believing something you shouldn't," Brooke continued before Nina could say anything. "I mean, it happened to me, remember?"

"It did?" Nina wrinkled her nose, thinking back over everything Brooke had ever posted. "You believed in ghosts?"

Brooke giggled. "Not ghosts," she said. Her voice went serious again. "But remember how I almost psyched myself out of staying at horse camp over the summer?"

"Yeah." Nina remembered that clearly. "You thought you and Foxy weren't good enough to ride with those snooty rich girls. Which was totally not the case, by the way."

"I know. You and Maddie and Haley helped me see that, and I ended up having a great time and made some incredible new friends," Brooke said. "But it's lucky I had you guys to talk sense into me, you know? Because at the beginning I was sure it wasn't going to work out, and once you start thinking that way, it can be really hard to stop." She hesitated again. "I'm worried that you might be doing that now."

"Oh." Nina sank down onto the edge of her bed and thought about that. Was Brooke right? Was she psyching herself out, blaming Serena for everything bad that happened?

Just then she heard her mother calling her name from the front of the house. Glancing at the clock, she realized it was time to leave for dinner.

"Listen, I have to go," she told Brooke. "My parents are waiting for me. But I'm really glad you called. You gave me lots to think about. Thanks."

"You're welcome," Brooke said. "Let me know what happens."

"You know I will." Nina said good-bye and hung up, hurrying for the door as her name rang through the house again.

Nina glanced at her wrist as she hurried into Cypress Trail Stables the next morning. Realizing she'd forgotten to put her watch on after her shower, she checked the barn's big, old-fashioned wall clock instead. Today was the grand opening of her mother's art show, but the gallery didn't open until noon. Even though Nina was already planning to head to the barn later for her ride with Jordan, she'd decided to come over and hand-graze Breezy for a few minutes. Living in tight city quarters, the pony didn't get as much time outside in the paddocks as Nina would have liked, so she tried to take him out for some grass as often as she could.

"Here I come, Breeze-man," she sang out as she hurried down the aisle toward her pony's stall. "Ready for a little of the green stuff? We won't have much time out there, but I know you'll—"

She cut herself off, stopping short in the doorway. The stall was empty.

"Breezy?" she said, glancing around as if expecting the pony to jump out of a shadowy corner. "Where are you?"

There was a clatter from around the corner of the aisle, and a moment later a wheelbarrow came into view. A barn worker, a young woman named Jane, was pushing it. She stopped when she saw Nina's face.

"Something wrong, Nina?" she said.

"Is Breezy out in a paddock?" Nina asked, realizing that had to be the answer. "Sorry for freaking out; it's just I know usually everyone stays in on Saturday mornings because of lessons, and—"

"That's right." Jane cut her off. "All the horses are in right now."

"They are?" Nina shot another look at Breezy's unoccupied stall, half expecting to see him looking out at her. "Um, Breezy's not in his stall."

"Oh." The young woman stepped over and looked into the stall. "That's odd. You don't think someone accidentally took him out to use in a lesson, do you?"

"He doesn't really look like any of the lesson horses," Nina said. "Maybe there's a new student who doesn't know any better, though—I'll check the rings. Thanks."

She rushed off before Jane could answer. There was

a big group lesson going on in the main ring, but it only took Nina a second to scan the horses and see that her pony wasn't among them. She turned and headed for the smaller ring. Miss Adaline was in there teaching a private lesson—a middle-aged woman on a large draft-cross mare who lived across the aisle from Breezy.

Nina clutched the rail, staring at the mare and trying not to panic. Miss Adaline noticed her and called for her student to halt.

"What's up, Nina?" the instructor asked, hurrying over. "Do you need me?"

"It's Breezy," Nina blurted out. "He's missing!"

"Missing?" Miss Adaline's forehead wrinkled beneath its fringe of dreads. "What are you talking about?"

"He's not in his stall. He's not in the big ring. And Jane says he's not in the paddocks."

Miss Adaline shrugged. "Well, he must be some-where," she said. "Someone would have called us if there was a loose pony wandering the park. Maybe someone moved him to clean his stall."

Nina hadn't thought about that. Sometimes the stall

cleaners shifted the horses around to make it easier to muck out the stalls.

"Thanks, that's probably it," she said with relief. "I'll check the stalls near his."

Still, she felt a little uneasy as she hurried back to the barn. Breezy knew she usually brought treats when she visited him. If he'd been in a stall nearby, wouldn't he have heard her voice and nickered to her as usual?

Trying not to think about that, she ducked down a side aisle as a shortcut back to the area of the barn where Breezy lived. Halfway down, she heard a familiar nicker and stopped stock-still.

"Breezy?" she blurted out, spinning around.

Sure enough, her pony's familiar spotted face was poking out over the half door of one of the stalls. Relief flooded through Nina, followed by confusion. What was Breezy doing way over here? This stall was nowhere near his own. Why would a stall cleaner walk him halfway across the barn when there were plenty of stalls closer, never mind several sets of crossties?

"Weird," she muttered. "But never mind. You're safe, and that's all that matters."

She rubbed the pony's face, then raced to the tack room for a lead rope. Soon she was leading Breezy out of the unfamiliar stall.

As he came out into the aisle, she glanced back at him— and stopped again, panic flooding through her at the sight of a huge, reddish smudge covering half of Breezy's side.

"Oh no—are you bleeding again?" she cried, flashing back to the morning she'd discovered that oozing cut on his nose. Dropping the lead rope, she darted to his side and searched for a cut or scrape.

But there was no sign of injury. And when Nina touched the smudge, she realized it wasn't even blood—it was more pinkish than the brownish-red of old blood or the bright red of fresh.

"Weird," she murmured again. "What did you get into, boy?"

She glanced into the stall, but there was nothing out of the ordinary in there. As she picked up the lead rope again, one of the other riding instructors appeared at the end of the aisle.

"Hey, Hector," Nina called. "Do you know how Breezy got over here?"

Hector came toward her, looking surprised. "Breezy was over here?" he said. "How'd that happen?"

"That's what I was asking you." Nina shrugged. "I just got here and found him in this stall."

The instructor scratched his head. "Beats me. He was in his normal stall when I helped the guys muck out a couple of hours ago."

"Oh. Okay, thanks." Nina swallowed hard as she glanced at her pony and the mysterious reddish mark on his side.

This is really weird, she thought. *But that doesn't mean it's Serena's work. Does it?*

• CHAPTER •
11

"AFTER YOU, LADIES." NINA'S FATHER HELD open the art gallery's glass door, gesturing for Nina and Delphine to go in.

Nina smiled briefly, but her mind wasn't really on her mom's art show. She couldn't stop thinking about what had happened with Breezy that morning. She'd gone around and asked every barn worker she could find, but nobody knew any more than Hector did about how the pony had ended up in the wrong part of the barn—or about what that strange pinkish mark on his side might be.

In the end, she'd barely had time to brush most of the

mark off his coat before it was time to go, though she'd promised the pony he would get his grazing time after her ride with Jordan later. She'd had to sprint home to have enough time to change clothes and then walk over to the gallery with her father and Delphine.

Her mother hurried to meet them as they entered. She'd been at the gallery since early that morning making sure everything was perfect for the grand opening. She looked perfect herself in a silk dress and a pair of vintage sandals Nina had given her for her last birthday.

"You're here!" she exclaimed. "I was starting to think you'd forgotten."

"Never!" Nina's father leaned down and kissed his wife. "We'd never miss your first big solo show."

Nina was glancing around the gallery. She'd seen most of the pieces before, but they looked different here somehow—bigger and more important. "Everything looks great, Mom," she said. "Wait, I almost forgot to ask which piece you picked to replace the one that got wrecked." Then her gaze fell on a piece she didn't recognize—a sculpture of a girl and a pony—and she gasped.

Her mother followed her gaze and smiled. "I was hoping you'd be so busy with your show and everything that you'd forget," she said. "I wanted it to be a surprise."

Nina stepped closer. The sculpture was modernist and stylized, like all her mother's work. But Nina had no trouble recognizing herself and Breezy. She was riding him bareback beneath a huge full moon.

"Wow," she breathed, stepping around and studying it from all angles. "This is amazing!"

Her mother smiled. "I call it *Moonlight Mile*," she said. "I can't believe I forgot about it for so long."

"We found it packed away in the crawl space," Nina's father put in. "When your mother hides a gift, she doesn't mess around."

Nina just nodded, still mesmerized by the sculpture. It was beautiful, but it was more than that—it really captured her bond with Breezy.

And that's what matters, she thought. *My relationship with Breezy. Not show ribbons, or silly superstitions about ghosts and curses. None of that is real*—this *is what's real.*

Then she flashed back to the weird pinkish mark on her

pony's coat that morning. That had been real too. Maybe she could write off the rest of the stuff that had happened to bad luck or an overactive imagination. Or psyching herself out, like Brooke seemed to think. But how had Breezy ended up in a distant stall with who knew what smudged all over him?

As she pondered that, she took a step backward to get a better look at the whole sculpture.

"Nina, look out!" her father exclaimed. He grabbed her arm and yanked her forward again just as Nina felt her arm hit something.

"Mon Dieu!" Delphine leaped over and steadied the sculpture that Nina had almost knocked over.

"Sorry!" Nina blurted out.

Her mother smiled and stepped over to adjust the sculpture. "No harm done. Besides, it's bronze—the floor's more likely to break than the piece."

Nina smiled weakly, glancing down at the gallery's pristine wooden floorboards. Her mother was probably right, but still . . .

The gallery owner hurried over and dragged Nina's

mother off to meet some important art critic who had just arrived. Nina barely saw her go. She was staring at the sculpture she'd almost crashed into, still shaking slightly from the close call.

Then she felt her father's hand on her shoulder. "You okay, Boo?" he asked. "You look pensive."

Nina forced a smile. "I'm fine."

"No, seriously." He peered into her face. "You haven't been yourself all day. All week, now that I think about it."

"It's nothing." Nina tried to smile, but it felt shaky. "Nothing real, anyway," she amended.

Her father cocked his head. "What do you mean?"

Nina glanced around. Delphine had wandered off to look at some of the other sculptures. Nobody else was nearby, though the gallery was filling up. Nina glanced at the *Moonlight Mile* sculpture again.

"It's just . . ." She bit her lip, not wanting her father to think she was going nuts.

But he won't think that, she reminded herself. *He wants to help me.*

"Boo?" he prompted, his expression so loving that it melted the last of Nina's hesitation.

"Okay," she said. "But you can't tell me I'm crazy, okay? See, it all started when I decided to dress up as Serena for the show. . . ."

The whole story poured out of her. Her father listened quietly, his expression impossible to read. When Nina had finished, he patted her arm.

"Meet me at the entrance," he said. "I'm just going to tell your mother we'll be back in a while."

"Where are we going?" Nina asked.

He smiled. "You'll see." Then he hurried off toward his wife.

A few minutes later, Nina and her father were back on their home block. He led the way toward his car, which was parked between a van and a fire hydrant.

"Climb in," he said, unlocking the doors.

Nina did as he said. "Are you going to tell me where we're going now?" she asked. "You're not planning to drop me off at the loony bin, are you?"

He chuckled. "Nope. You'll see."

Nina fidgeted in her seat as they set off. She watched the familiar city streets slide by outside the window, trying to figure out where they were going.

When they passed the Superdome and then the edge of the French Quarter, she started to have an inkling. She nodded as her father pulled into a parking spot just off Basin Street.

"The cemetery," she guessed as they climbed out of the car. "St. Louis? We're going there?"

"Come with me." Her father smiled and strode off.

Inside the cemetery, her father paused, glancing around. Then he nodded and started walking.

Nina followed. Finally they stopped in front of a modest crypt.

"Here we are," her father said, waving an arm.

Nina stepped closer, leaning down for a better look at the stone. There was no name on it, just an etched image. It was faded almost smooth with time, but after a moment Nina figured out what it was.

"A horse?" she said. "I think it's a horse."

"It is," her father confirmed.

"That's cool," Nina said. "But why . . ."

"This is Serena's grave," her father said. "Your uncle Oscar did some research when he was in school and figured it out."

"Oh!" Nina shook her head. "No wonder Jordan and I couldn't find it. It doesn't even have her name on it."

Her father nodded. "Oscar's research also revealed that Serena was known in her time as an outstanding horsewoman," he said. "Apparently she had a special rapport with horses and rode better than any man in New Orleans." He winked. "Remind you of anyone?"

Nina smiled. "Wow. I guess loving horses runs in the family."

"Uh-huh." Her father glanced at the etching. "Serena had some good things in her life. But like everyone, she had some bad luck too."

"Her fiancé's death," Nina said.

"Yes. It's too bad she let that one piece of bad luck ruin her whole life." Her father shot Nina a sidelong glance. "She focused so much on what she'd lost that she forgot to appreciate everything else she had, w.

helped her through the tragedy."

Nina nodded, pretty sure she knew what her father was trying to tell her. Serena had gotten so fixated on what had gone wrong that it had taken her over and made her miserable. Was Nina doing the same thing by worrying too much about her recent run of bad luck?

Nothing that's happened to me is half as bad as what happened to Serena, she thought. *Still, maybe I am losing perspective a little. At least Brooke seems to think so, and now Dad, too.*

"Can I have a minute alone with Serena?" she asked quietly.

Her father nodded. "I'll meet you by the entrance whenever you're ready." He leaned over and kissed the top of her head, then hurried off.

Nina crouched in front of the grave, staring at the horse etching. "Serena," she said. "It's me—your great-great-great-great-niece. I love horses too."

She paused, feeling a little foolish for talking to a

voman who'd been dead for well over a hundred years. But she shrugged and continued.

"These days, there aren't as many horses around New Orleans as there were in your time," she said. "But I'm really lucky, because I have a super-special Chincoteague pony. His name is Breezy, and he's about as perfect as a pony can be." Remembering some of the issues they'd had at the show, she added, "At least he is when I remember to ride my best. And sometimes even when I don't." She laughed. "Anyway, it's because of Breezy that I met some awesome friends online. . . ."

She went on to tell Serena about the Pony Post. After that she talked a little about the horse show. She was just describing her mother's *Moonlight Mile* sculpture when she caught movement out of the corner of her eye.

Glancing that way, she realized a tour group was looking at a large mausoleum nearby. Nina blushed, wondering if they were close enough to have heard her talking to the gravestone.

Who cares if they did? she thought. *This is important.*

"Anyway," she told Serena softly, "I'm really sorry if I

insulted you by dressing up as you for the costume class. But it wasn't meant like that. Especially now that I know we had a love of horses in common, you know?"

She paused, as if expecting Serena to answer. Then she laughed and patted the etched stone.

"Thanks for the chat," she said. "I'd better go."

She stood up, ignoring a little kid from the tour group who was staring at her. Already feeling better, she hurried to meet her father.

◆ CHAPTER ◆

12

NINA PICKED HER WAY THROUGH THE crowded art gallery, saying hello to people she knew and smiling at everyone else. It was almost four o'clock, and it seemed that just about everyone Nina had ever met had come out to support her mother's show. Most of her local relatives were there, along with various friends and neighbors.

"Nina!" her mother said when she noticed her approaching. "You're still here. Aren't you riding with Jordan this afternoon?"

"I was about to leave," Nina said. "I just wanted to let you know—and to say congrats." She glanced around the busy room. "I'm really proud of you, Mom."

"Thanks." Her mother beamed. "I feel really lucky—especially to have such a terrific daughter."

They hugged; then someone else called Nina's mother's name, wanting to talk to her. Nina waved and headed for the door.

She walked home as quickly as she could. She'd laid out her riding clothes that morning, so it only took a moment to pull them on. But she'd forgotten to put out socks.

She opened a drawer to grab some. As she did, she noticed the paper bag she'd shoved in there the day before.

She picked it up and pulled out the voodoo doll. She'd almost forgotten about it. After her talks with her father, Brooke, and Serena, she felt a little foolish about having been pressured into buying it.

Then again, maybe it hadn't been a waste. Voodoo powers might not be real, but voodoo was an interesting tradition—just like her family history. Maybe it would be fun to honor that. . . .

Nina unfolded the pamphlet that had come with the doll and scanned the section on good voodoo. She found a healing spell that sounded simple and didn't require any ingredients beyond the subject's name and a candle, which Madame Marceline had included in the package.

Still feeling slightly foolish, Nina wrote Serena's name on the doll, then lit the candle and intoned the words from the pamphlet. When she finished, she waited a moment, as if expecting something to happen: a puff of smoke, a ghostly visitation, or . . .?

Finally she smiled and blew out the candle. "There," she said, propping the doll up on the shelf beside her copy of *Misty of Chincoteague*. "Can't hurt to put some good energy out into the universe, right?"

Her smile faded a little when that morning's mysterious stall switch popped into her mind. It was the one thing that still didn't have a rational explanation she could figure out. But she shook off the thought, pulling on her socks and heading for the door.

When she got to the barn, Jordan was already picking out Freckles's feet in the crossties near Breezy's stall. "Hey," Jordan said. "I was about to text and see if you were still coming."

"Sorry I'm late." Nina rubbed Breezy's nose as he stuck

his head into the aisle and nickered. "I was having fun at Mom's art show and lost track of time."

Jordan finished picking out Freckles's left hind hoof and let the foot drop. Then she straightened up and looked at Nina. "Did you decide what to do about . . ." She glanced around and lowered her voice. "You know, the voodoo stuff?"

Nina smiled. "I'm pretty sure Serena won't be bothering us anymore," she said. "But it's got nothing to do with voodoo or any other spooky stuff like that."

"What do you mean?" Jordan asked.

"I mean I'm pretty sure Serena wasn't actually behind any of the weird stuff that's been happening to me lately," Nina said. "Brooke and my dad helped me see that."

"Brooke? Who's—oh wait, one of your imaginary friends, right?"

"Yeah. Anyway, she helped me figure out that I was letting my imagination run away with me when I knew very well that ghosts aren't real and everything that happened had another explanation. Like Breezy was spookier than usual because he was hyped up from the show. He stopped at that jump because I was riding like a space cadet." She felt a blush creep over her cheeks as she thought about the next explanation. "Uh, and my pants split because they were old."

Just then Miss Adaline came into view at the end of the aisle. When she saw Nina, she hurried over.

"Listen, Nina," the instructor said. "We're still trying to figure out what happened with Breezy's stall and the rest this morning. Nobody's admitted to moving him yet, but we're going to keep looking into it until we figure it out."

"Okay," Nina said. "Thanks."

As Miss Adaline hurried off, Jordan stared at Nina. "What was that all about?"

Nina told her what had happened that morning. Jordan's eyes grew wider and wider with alarm.

"Oh my gosh!" she exclaimed. "And you still don't think Serena could be real? I mean, how else can you explain it? Plus you had all those creepy dreams, remember? That had to be Serena too, right?"

"Not necessarily," Nina said. "I always have vivid dreams during a full moon. And it only makes sense that

I'd dream about whatever was on my mind at the time—in this case, Serena." She shrugged. "As for the stall switch, well, who knows. But I'm sure they'll figure it out."

Jordan didn't look so sure. But before she could say anything, Brett turned the corner and came their way.

"What are you doing here?" Jordan asked her brother.

Nina was wondering the same thing. Brett grinned at both of them.

"I was just in the neighborhood," he said. "Figured I'd stop by and make sure you guys were staying out of trouble.

Jordan rolled her eyes. "No, seriously. What do you want?"

"Um . . ." Brett reached into his backpack and pulled out a water bottle. "I brought you this. You know, it's important to stay hydrated, Sis."

Now Jordan looked irritated. "Are you spying on us or something? Because if you are, I'm so telling Mom. . . ."

Nina felt her new sense of peace waver. Okay, so maybe the vintage breeches had split because the thread was old and rotted and not because Serena was trying to punish her. But what difference did it make why it had happened? Brett still thought she was a dolt.

Then he turned to face her. "Okay, I admit it—I didn't really come to bring my sister water," he said. "I don't care if she's hydrated or not."

"Gee, thanks a lot," Jordan said.

Brett ignored her, instead staring at the air somewhere near Nina's left ear. "Uh, I came to tell you something," he blurted out. "I, um, might have messed with your runt pony this morning?"

"What?" Nina stared at him in confusion.

He shrugged, shoving his hands in his pockets and shifting his weight from one leg to the other. "It was supposed to be, you know, a joke?" he mumbled. "I heard Jordan telling Mom about your ghost cousin or whatever, and I thought it'd be funny. . . ."

"What did you do?" Jordan demanded, glaring at him.

"Nothing that bad," he replied defensively. "I used Mom's lipstick to write 'Beware!' on the runt's side in this ghostly writing." He glanced at Breezy. "But then he rolled around and smudged it, so I tried to wash it off with the hose. But someone was coming before I could finish, so I just stuck him in a stall and took off." He glanced at Nina. "Sorry."

Nina couldn't answer for a moment. For a second she was angry. Did Brett even realize how worried she'd been? Had he even thought about how Breezy could have been hurt by being stuck in some strange stall?

She knew the answer: No. Of course not. How could he know any of that?

"It's okay," she told him, realizing what this meant. Serena was off the hook for real. There was a rational explanation for everything that had happened—just as Nina should have trusted from the start.

"You sure?" Brett said cautiously. "You're not mad?"

"Maybe a little," she told him. "But you can make it up to me by promising two things."

"What?" He sounded even more cautious now.

"First, you have to stop calling Breezy a runt," Nina said. "It hurts his feelings."

Brett rolled his eyes, but he nodded. "Done. What's the second thing?"

Nina shot a mischievous look at Jordan. "Second, you have to rent a horse and ride out with us today," she said.

"What?" Brett and Jordan exclaimed at the same time.

"That way, you'll realize that riding really is a sport," Nina went on, smiling for real now. "Maybe you'll even figure out how fun it is."

Brett hesitated, glancing at Freckles and then at Breezy. "Okay," he said. "No biggie. Who do I need to talk to about that?"

Nina's father looked up from the TV when she came in later. "Hey," he said, hitting the mute button. "How was your ride?"

"Good." Nina flopped into a chair. "You know Jordan's brother, Brett? He came with us."

"Really? I didn't know he was a rider," her father said.

"He isn't. Or at least he wasn't." Nina smiled, thinking back over the ride. Brett had been nervous at first, but he'd caught on to the basics quickly, and the barn's oldest and calmest lesson horse had taken good care of him during the ride. "But I think he might start trail riding with us sometimes now. We had a really fun time." Seeing her father's eyebrows raise slightly, she quickly added, "All three of us."

"Hmm." Her father stood up. "Why don't you tell me more about it while we start dinner? Your mom's in the shower and I know she's exhausted."

"Sure," Nina said. "Just let me change out of my riding clothes."

It was pretty late by the time Nina headed to bed. Kim, DeeDee, and Tim had stopped by while she and her father were cooking, and they'd all ended up staying for dinner. The group had had a great time talking about the art-show opening, which had been a huge success. Nina's mother had reported that several people had expressed an interest in buying *Moonlight Mile*, though Nina was glad to hear that her mom had explained that that particular piece wasn't for sale.

She logged on to the Pony Post and found several messages from her friends.

[BROOKE] Hi all! Just checking in to
see if Nina posted anything about
the art show. How'd it go N?

[MADDIE] I was wondering that too. Also, did
u all ride today? Cloudy and I had a lesson.
Good news? Lesson was great! Bad news?
I busted my reins b/c I dropped them after I
got off and she stepped on them. Grr! Good
thing my b'day is coming up soon . . .

[HALEY] Sry about yr reins Mads! It was
icy here today, so I cleaned tack instead
of riding. Can't wait for real snow!

[MADDIE] Brrr—Snow? Ice? it all
sounds cold to me! lol!

Nina shivered too. It almost never snowed in New
Orleans, though she'd experienced real snowfalls a couple
of times while visiting her mother's side of the family in

New Jersey and Pennsylvania. She glanced at the moon rising in the warm night sky outside, then opened a text box.

[NINA] Hi all! Art show was stupendous—about a zillion people came, and Mom is super happy. Yay! Also, I figured out something important, thanks to a certain Brooke (and my dad, and my own brain). Serena wasn't haunting me after all! (I know, I know, you guys knew it all along, lol!) I'm happy about that, esp. b/c it means I can go back to enjoying my fave family legend. (And my super cool pony!) Anyway, I'll tell u more about the art show and post some pics tmw—right now I'm falling asleep on the keyboard, ha ha! Sweet dreams, all!

She logged off and set the computer on her desk. On her way past, she paused just long enough to pat the voodoo doll on the bookshelf. Then she climbed into bed and glanced at the moon once more before closing her eyes, smiling as she wondered if Serena would visit her dreams that night.

✦ Glossary ✦

Chincoteague pony: A breed of pony found on Assateague Island, which lies off the coasts of Maryland and Virginia. Chincoteague ponies are sometimes referred to as wild horses, but are more properly called "feral" since they are not native to the island but were brought there by humans sometime many years past. There are several theories about how this might have happened, including the one told in the classic novel *Misty of Chincoteague* by Marguerite Henry. That novel also details the world-famous pony swim and auction that still take place in the town of Chincoteague to this day.

Appaloosa: A breed of horse most recognized by its several distinctive spotted coat patterns. The breed was developed in the 1700s by the Nez Perce tribe of Native Americans, and is popular to this day in Western riding and many other disciplines. It is the official state horse of Idaho.

cross rail: A type of jump in which two poles are crisscrossed to form an X. Cross rails are often used for horses and riders who are just learning to jump, due to their (usually) low height and inviting shape.

flat class: There are various types of flat classes at different types of horse shows; however, in a hunter show like the one in this book, a flat class could also be called an "under saddle" class. It's a group class in which horses are judged on the quality of their gaits (walk, trot, and canter). At a student show, the judge might also take a horse's manners and suitability into account.

hunter competition: A type of English horse show in which horses are judged on their form over fences and quality of movement. Hunter classes were originally developed to show off horses used for fox hunting, though there is little overlap between modern American show hunters and field hunters.

mounting block: This term can refer to any object a rider steps onto to mount a horse, from a specially made step-shaped block to a stump, boulder, or truck tailgate. While many riders can and do mount directly from the ground, a mounting block helps to minimize wear and tear on the horse's back as well as the rider's tack.

opening circle: Sometimes called a "hunter circle" or "courtesy circle," this is when a horse and rider trot and/or canter a circle before beginning a course of jumps. It helps to establish the proper pace for the round.

paddock: In the United States and Canada, this term usually refers to a relatively small enclosure for horses. A larger enclosure would normally be called a pasture.

saddle seat: This is a particular type of English riding developed mainly on plantations in the American South. Saddle seat riders normally prefer breeds with an upright neck carriage and a flashy, high-stepping trot, including the American Saddlebred, the Tennessee Walking Horse, the Morgan horse, and others.

sidesaddle: This form of riding was developed in the Middle Ages as a way for women to ride modestly in a skirt. The rider sits with both legs on one side of the horse, instead of astride. There are special saddles used to make this easier, and even today sidesaddle classes at shows are popular with competitors and spectators alike.

warm-up ring: A separate ring set aside at a horse show where competitors can warm up before their classes.

Marguerite Henry's Ponies of Chincoteague is inspired by the award-winning books by Marguerite Henry, the beloved author of such classic horse stories as *King of the Wind*; *Misty of Chincoteague*; *Justin Morgan Had a Horse*; *Stormy, Misty's Foal*; *Misty's Twilight*; and *Album of Horses*, among many other titles.

Learn more about the world of Marguerite Henry at www.MistyofChincoteague.org.

Don't miss the
next book in the series!

Book 5: *A Winning Gift*

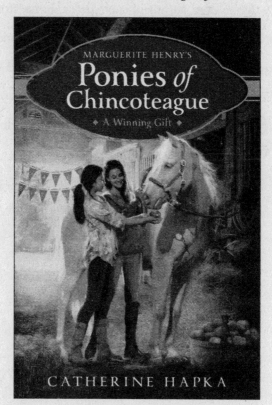